TORI MITCHELL

Hometown Hero
in Sunset Cove

Sixth Street Books

Copyright © 2024 by Tori Mitchell

All rights reserved.

No part of this publication may be reproduced, distributed, or transmitted in any form or by any means, including photocopying, recording, or other electronic or mechanical methods, without the prior written permission of the publisher, except as permitted by U.S. copyright law.

This is a work of fiction. All characters, places, and events are products of the author's imagination or used in a fictitious manner. Any resemblance to actual persons (living or deceased) is coincidental.

Books written by Tori Mitchell

The Sunset Cove Series
Coming Home to Sunset Cove
Second Chances in Sunset Cove
Hometown Hero in Sunset Cove
Christmas in Sunset Cove
Finding Home in Sunset Cove

Sunset Cove Shorts
(July 2025 novellas)
The Christmas Inheritance
The Christmas Gift
The Christmas Surprise

Chapter One

Rachel

Rachel Lancaster sorted through the chaos on her desk. Her phone was somewhere in this pile. It had to be.

She shuffled through tests to be graded, spare xylophone mallets, and sheet music for next month's concert.

No phone.

Rachel growled in frustration and resisted the urge to shove the contents of her desk onto the floor. Making a bigger mess wouldn't solve anything. She needed to calm down and think.

She tried to visualize where her phone might be, picturing each class throughout the day.

That's right. She used her phone to play music for her kindergarten class. Rachel grinned as she marched to the front of the classroom and grabbed her phone.

She held it up in triumph and wondered why she'd been so flustered. Her sense of victory faded as she remembered her end goal—she needed advice from a friend. Rachel was meeting Dr. Scott Hart for lunch in thirty minutes, and it had been a long time since her last lunch date.

Parent meetings didn't count.

Rachel pulled up her contact information and tapped on the icon for Brook Reed. Her best friend's bakery was slow around lunchtime, and she should be able to talk.

Straight to the point, Rachel launched into questions as soon as her friend answered the phone. "This is a business lunch, right? He's not interested in dating."

Brook chuckled as a timer went off inside the bakery. "'Hello' to you, too. It *sounds* like a business lunch, but Dr. Hart seems interested in you, too. He should be interested. You're single, gorgeous, and fun to be around."

Rachel let the line go silent as Brook opened an oven door. The clatter of metal trays told her she'd have a moment to collect her thoughts.

She glanced at her reflection in the classroom window. Her, attractive? Rachel wasn't so sure. She couldn't see past her frizzy hair and tired eyes.

Rachel worked long hours as the school's only music teacher. She didn't mind, but sometimes it felt like she used work to fill a family-sized gap in her life. She didn't have family in the area. Just some great friends.

Rachel loved kids, but what could she do about it? Most men her age either had families already, or ran away at the mention of children. She was too busy to commit to a long-term relationship. At thirty-four, her chances of starting a family were slipping away.

Brook cleared her throat. "Are you there? Sorry about that. The muffins were done."

"Still here." Rachel sighed and moved away from the window. "Still nervous."

"Stop being nervous. You're an attractive, single woman. He's an attractive guy who asked you out for lunch. Have some fun. What are you worried about?"

Rachel bit back a laugh. Sure, Brook had nothing to worry about. She was all but engaged to Brad Brown. Rachel was certain there would be another wedding in town soon. All of her friends were getting married.

They were still her friends, married or not—but things changed. Priorities shifted. People got left behind. Not that she minded, of course. She wanted her friends to be happy.

Time to change the subject.

"I want to make sure we're reading this correctly," Rachel said, using her best I'm-in-charge teacher voice. "Dr. Hart wants to discuss the hospital fundraiser. We're meeting at the hospital cafeteria. It'll be crowded and noisy. Nothing intimate about it."

"Suit yourself. Dr. Hart was cute." Brook paused again, but there were muffled sounds in the background. She sighed. "I've got to go. I have to cover the front register, but call me if you need anything." Her friend's cheerful demeanor turned stern. "And I want updates. Don't forget to stop by the bakery after school."

Rachel could imagine Brook wiggling her eyebrows. Her friend always wanted details.

Was Dr. Hart really interested in her? They'd only met once, in the emergency room, when Brook's fiance broke his ankle. The doctor had asked for her phone number as they left the hospital. He seemed interested in her connections at the school.

Still, Brook had a point. The doctor was very attractive—especially when he smiled. Rachel tried to ignore the butterflies in her stomach as she thought about his dimpled grin.

They were getting together for a fundraiser, but did she need to look tired and drab when they met? It couldn't hurt to make a positive impression.

Rachel dashed to the closet and grabbed her purse. She pulled out a brush and her emergency makeup bag. Using the camera on her phone as a mirror, she applied a fresh coat of mascara and a swipe of the lipstick from her bag. The lipstick was a little dry, she noted, rubbing her lips together. Might be time to replace that tube.

She chuckled to herself. Rachel couldn't remember the last time she'd used lipstick, let alone how long that tube had been in her bag. She dressed nice enough, but her appearance at work wasn't a priority. Six-year-olds cared about how you treated them. They didn't notice if you used this month's on-trend eyeliner.

Rachel was packing up and settling her nerves when there was a soft knock. One of her students stood outside the door.

Emily Wilde was one of her best music students, and one of the nicest, too. The fourth grader had moved to Sunset Cove this year. She'd quickly won over her teachers' hearts. Rachel couldn't rush such a sweet student away. "Hi, Emily. What do you need?"

Emily smiled uncertainly. "I'm sorry to bug you, Ms. Lancaster. I lost my recorder at my dad's house. Do you have any extras? I don't want to stop practicing."

Rachel's heart warmed. The fourth graders were having a recorder concert for their parents soon. For many of these kids, it would be their first time performing in front of others. Nerves were running high.

"I've only got three recorders left. Try to find the one you took home," Rachel warned her, handing Emily the slim, white instrument. She warmed her warning with a smile. "I'm glad you're practicing, though. You're doing a wonderful job."

The girl grinned as she reached for the recorder, showing a gap where one of her last baby teeth had fallen out. "Thanks. Mom says I'm doing good. I can play Ode to Joy and Hot Cross Buns. I've still got to learn the other two songs."

"You've got lots of time. Just keep practicing." Rachel cheered on the girl as she picked up her purse. "Now, do you need a hall pass? Or could I walk you to class? I'm leaving for my lunch break now."

They walked down the hall together, and Rachel left Emily in her classroom with a quick wave. Then she speed-walked out of the building and into her car.

Rachel thought back to her conversation with Emily and smiled. It made her happy to get students excited about music, even if most of them wouldn't play instruments again after fourth grade.

Emily had distracted Rachel from her nerves. She shifted the car into drive and headed toward Sunset County's only hospital. Rachel still wasn't sure if this was a working lunch—or the start of something with Dr. Hart. But she was about to find out.

Rachel glanced at the clock in her car. She was only running two minutes late. For Rachel, that was practically on time.

Chapter Two

Scott

Dr. Scott Hart glanced at his watch. He had ten minutes until his meeting with Rachel Lancaster.

Best to leave now. If someone saw him outside a patient's room, they would pull Scott aside and keep him on the floor. He couldn't be late for their first meeting.

His pediatric nurse walked in as Scott gathered up his papers. "Good, you're still here. I've got two discharges ready. Let's send these kids home before your meeting."

Bless his heart, Adam Locke was efficient. Adam had been his first new hire for the children's pediatric division of Sunset Cove Community Hospital. He was an excellent nurse, great with kids, and a fantastic co-worker.

Scott grabbed his laptop and nodded. "The timing's perfect. I was just about to leave. Madison's bloodwork came back normal, and Dominic's keeping food down?"

"Right on both counts. They're both ready to go home. Their parents are eager to leave, too."

Scott clicked through their files, digitally signing both discharge papers. He closed the laptop with a nod. "My lunch meeting shouldn't be too long. Text me if it's urgent."

Adam checked his watch. "That's fine. We're waiting for two patients' test results. They'll be back by the time you're done. Enjoy your lunch."

Satisfied with his morning's work, Scott picked up his papers and strolled out of the office.

The CEO of the hospital, Dr. William Stewart, was standing outside the elevator. He reached out to give Scott a firm handshake and patted him on the shoulder. "How's our top pediatric physician?"

Scott chuckled and returned the greeting. "I'm your only pediatric physician, but not for long. I'm meeting with a member of my fundraising team today."

"Excellent. Who are you meeting with?"

Scott quickly checked the elevator to see if the "down" button was lit. "Her name is Rachel Lancaster. She's a music teacher at Sunset Elementary. I'd like her to put on a small concert during the gala."

William raised his eyebrows. "A concert with elementary school kids? This is a high-dollar fundraiser."

Scott had expected some pushback. He would still hire an orchestra to entertain their guests—or at least a string quartet. But every party had music. This gala needed to showcase the community's kids. Show people why donations were so important.

This night wasn't about fancy food or hiring the best violinist in the state. They were making better medical care possible for the children in the community. Shouldn't those children be involved in the process?

Still, Scott had hoped to discuss his ideas with Rachel before pitching anything to the hospital board.

Instead, he'd need to rely on his skills from the emergency room and think on his feet. As the men entered the elevator, Scott took a moment to analyze the facts. William had hired Scott for his medical and personal skills, and the CEO supported most of his ideas. Time to commit.

"Yes, sir. We're discussing a children's choir. Something small to entertain the crowd before the silent auction ends. Inspire people to support the pediatric wing, and showcase the children who will benefit. I was planning to discuss the details with Rachel today and contact you soon."

To Scott's delight, his CEO's eyes lit up with enthusiasm. "It's a brilliant idea. A children's choir! Featuring the children in our town! Meet with this teacher and report back by next week. We'll finalize our plans and get this idea past the board."

The elevator stopped at the second floor, one level above the cafeteria. But instead of exiting, William held his hand over the door to stop it from closing. "And how are you doing, Scott? Enjoying life in Sunset Cove?"

Scott nodded. "I've only lived in New Jersey for six months, but I like the town. It's quiet. You've got a strong staff, with lots of room for growth. I'm glad I took this assignment."

"It's quiet now. Wait until the ocean warms up." William chuckled. "June brings tourists with sprained ankles and jellyfish stings. We'll see how you feel about Sunset Cove by the end of summer. I hope you'll stay, though. You're making a difference already, and I want you here during interviews when we staff the new unit. You'll be a big help there, too."

William took another step toward the elevator door. "Any girlfriends here or back home? Just wondering what might impact your decision to stay long term."

"No, sir. I've got enough on my plate. I like an uncomplicated life."

"Don't we all? Just be careful. This town's got a lot of heart. We've got a lot of good women, too." William chuckled again. "I met my wife in Sunset Cove forty years ago. I'd planned to move on to a bigger hospital, but stayed for her. Life has a funny way of becoming complicated."

The CEO held out his hand for another shake and pumped Scott's arm. "Great to see you again, Dr. Hart. I look forward to hearing about your children's choir."

William let the elevator door close behind him, leaving Scott alone. That had gone better than expected. At least one member of the board would back his plans. Now he had to make it downstairs to meet with Rachel.

Scott smiled as the elevator doors opened on the first floor. He checked his watch again. Right on time. Scott walked out of the elevator and headed toward the cafeteria.

He shook his head as he thought about the CEO's warning. A girlfriend? Rachel was pretty, but who had time for a girlfriend? He had a pediatric ward to build.

Chapter Three

Rachel

Rachel hesitated outside the hospital cafeteria's heavy doors.

She glanced at her reflection in a nearby window and smoothed her hair, then tugged at her dress. This was as fancy as she got on a school day. Hopefully, it was enough to make a positive impression.

This wasn't the first time they'd met, of course. But surely Dr Hart wouldn't judge what she'd worn to the emergency room last month.

She stopped fidgeting and reached for the door. A large hand grabbed the handle before her.

"Allow me," a deep voice said.

Rachel glanced up. Her eyes continued traveling upward until she made eye contact with Dr. Scott Hart. She'd forgotten how tall he was. Even in heels, Rachel barely came to his shoulders.

Her heart beat faster as she looked up at him. Rachel was used to being the shortest person in the room, but Scott's towering presence intimidated her.

She told her heart to slow down and stop being so silly.

Intimidated or not, they'd be working together for the foreseeable future. Time to play it cool. Pretending that Dr. Hart was just another one of her students' parents, she gave a wide smile and nodded. She allowed him to hold the door open while she walked through it.

Once they were inside, she reached up to shake his hand. "Dr. Hart. It's a pleasure to meet you again, especially under better circumstances."

"Yes, it's nice to meet people outside a medical setting. And please, call me Scott." He returned her grin, making him look more friendly and approachable. "I'm only a doctor when I'm wearing the white coat."

Rachel choked back a laugh. Tall and handsome, plus a sense of humor? Maybe she was more intrigued than intimidated. Brook would be thrilled. "Thanks for texting me, Scott. I'm not sure how I can help with your fundraiser, but I'm flattered you asked."

Scott led them to a back corner. Since it was only eleven o'clock, most of the tables were still empty. So much for meeting in a loud, impersonal cafeteria.

Her heart gave a little flutter as Scott pulled out a chair and gestured for her to sit. What if Brook was right, and this was a date?

Scott sat in his own seat and pulled out a thick folder, crushing her hopes and clearing any confusion. Not a date. Definitely a business meeting. She mentally kicked herself for getting ideas. Frizzy music teachers didn't attract handsome doctors, no matter how nice they seemed.

Scott cleared his throat and set his phone on top of the folder. "The staff orders food through an app. They'll text me when it's ready. What would you like? My treat."

Rachel searched for a menu, then peeked around at the other diners' food. A salad at the next table looked delicious. "I'll have a grilled chicken salad, please. Ranch dressing."

He nodded and picked up his phone to open the cafeteria's app. "Good choice. The salads are phenomenal here." He finished placing the order, then opened his folder to show a thick pile of spreadsheets and notes. "Shall we start? Our food will be ready soon."

"Of course. Can you tell me about this fundraiser? You're building a new pediatric wing. I'm guessing you need to raise money for that."

"That's right." Scott reached into his folder and pulled out some handwritten notes. "We're hosting a charity gala in three months. I need to finalize the entertainment and theme for the night, and I'd like to include the children who will benefit from the expansion. Give people a reason to support the hospital. When I realized you were a music teacher, things clicked into place."

Scott looked at her intently and folded his hands on the table. "I'd like you to gather a children's choir. Nothing too large. Two or three dozen children. The younger kids sound so sweet when they sing."

Rachel's jaw dropped. Forget being attracted to the man. Was he crazy? Sunset Elementary didn't have a choir. They started band and chorus in middle school.

She closed her mouth and frowned. "It's a lovely idea, but you've got the wrong age group. I'm happy to connect you with our middle school choir director. Or one of the local churches could volunteer their youth choir? The pastor at Grace Lutheran is very passionate about community involvement." Her voice rose with nerves as she spoke, nearly squeaking by the time she was done. He was asking the wrong person for help.

To her surprise, Scott just smiled and pulled a stack of papers out of his folder. "I did some research. The Children's Hospital of Phoenix did a fundraiser with local students singing. It raised more money than any fundraiser they've ever done. And look at this article. Last year, an elementary school in California needed a new roof. Their students put on a concert. They earned enough money to replace the roof *and* double the number of books in their school library."

He closed his folder and handed the articles to Rachel. "This will work, and you're the right teacher for the job. I talked to a few staff members with younger children. You bring out your students' passion for music, and that's what we need. Professional musicians are wonderful, but enthusiastic, local children will show our donors why they need to support this hospital." He looked Rachel in the eyes, challenging her. "Are you in?"

Rachel's face flushed with heat as she glanced through the articles. She hadn't realized parents spoke so highly of her. Scott had a point, though. The children of Sunset Cove would benefit the most, so it made sense to include them.

She thought of her students and sat straighter. Rachel would do almost anything for her students—even something big and new like this. "I'm flattered. If I can gather enough children, I'll do it. I need a few days to gauge the students' interest."

"Fair enough. You've got my phone number. Let me know by next week. My CEO is looking for an update."

"That should be enough time." She handed back the articles and tilted her head in question. "You've put some thought into this. What made you go into medicine instead of marketing? You seem suited for it."

Scott grinned as his phone chimed. "I'll take that as a compliment. I just moved to Sunset Cove. Once the dust settles, I'll be head of the new children's division. My job is to raise money, hire staff, and steer this hospital into the future. As a doctor, I can only help one child at a time. As the new director, I'll help an entire community." He held up his phone. "Give me a minute. Our salads are ready."

Rachel mulled over Scott's response as he went to get their food. His answer impressed her. She'd gone into teaching for the same reasons. Parents got to influence one child's life—a few children, if you were lucky. But teachers touch the lives of hundreds of students each year. She loved her job, even if it wasn't always easy.

Her mouth watered as Scott set a grilled chicken salad in front of her. She'd run out of her apartment without breakfast again today. Her lunch break was so early in the day that she often slept in, rather than fussing with a morning meal.

Scott placed a napkin in his lap and cracked open the lid on his salad dressing. "What got you into teaching? And more importantly, what convinced you to help with the fundraiser? You seemed hesitant. I need to know if you're uncomfortable. We're a team now."

Rachel's face heated again. She hadn't realized her reluctance was so obvious. She still wasn't sure if she was the right person for the job, but she'd do her best—for her students' sake. "I became a teacher because I love music, and I love children."

Rachel hesitated, gathering her thoughts. She was far out of her comfort zone with this fundraiser, yet she'd barely hesitated to agree. Why? "Our town had two children go through chemotherapy last year. A toddler and one of my students. The treatments for cancer are tough enough, but both girls' parents missed work to travel back and forth to Children's Hospital of Philadelphia. Things would have been easier if they'd gotten treatment here in town. If this can make one family's life easier, I'll do everything in my power to help."

Scott speared a piece of chicken and chewed thoughtfully. "We don't have a pediatric oncologist on our recruitment list yet. But I'm hoping to build connections with the cancer centers at larger children's hospitals. Children would still be diagnosed at CHOP, but they could set up a chemotherapy schedule at home. Less traveling for treatment. There's a lot of work to do before that happens, but it's one of my biggest goals."

Rachel's eyes watered at the idea of making a child's journey easier. She'd worked with the Sunset Cove Kindness Committee to collect gas cards and meals for Aubrey O'Grady's family, and knew how much they'd struggled. The commute to Philadelphia had been hard on the fourth grader and her parents.

Scott's face showed nothing but compassion, she noted. He clearly cared about his patients.

"Like I said, give me a few days," said Rachel. "I'll do my best to gather enough kids for a choir. I want to help."

Rachel walked out of the hospital with a spring in her step. No, this hadn't been a date. Scott didn't seem interested in her, but that was okay. They'd make a good team, and they'd make a big difference in this town.

She wasn't a mother, but Rachel was a Mama Bear for every one of her students. Time to fight for their right to have better medical care.

Chapter Four

Scott

Scott finished ordering a breathing treatment for his youngest patient of the day. He submitted the order to the pharmacy, then turned to give the child's mother a reassuring smile. "He'll feel better soon. I ordered his medication. The nurse should be here in a few minutes."

He left the toddler sitting on an adult-sized emergency room bed.

Scott was the first pediatric physician at Sunset Cove Community Hospital, but he wouldn't be the last. That's why this year's fundraiser was so important. They needed more space to take care of kids, in a setup designed for children—smaller beds, right-sized tools, colorful walls, and an area separate from adult problems.

More importantly, they needed nurses and doctors who could care for tiny patients with big fears. Adam, their first pediatric nurse, was a great start.

The gala would determine how quickly they could build their pediatric wing, and how soon they would be fully staffed. Every growing hospital had the same struggles. They might have lofty goals and construction projects, but they couldn't do anything without community support.

Scott felt a familiar buzz of excitement when he considered the hospital's future. He could make a real difference here. Unfortunately, everything came down to money. Even a hospital like

CHOP couldn't survive and expand without private donations. Scott loved medicine, but he'd never planned to earn an honorary business degree on top of his M.D.

Rachel was right, though. He was good at this. He enjoyed helping Sunset Cove's small hospital expand to meet its community's needs.

Scott grinned as he thought about Rachel. They'd make a great team. It wasn't hard to spend time with her, either.

He worked with women doctors and nurses, but they'd never been more than co-workers. Rachel was different. She had a sparkle in her eyes that invited you to lean closer. Talk longer. Even the way she walked was different. Instead of the brisk steps most doctors took to rush from task to task, Rachel walked like she could break into dance at any moment.

Her way of talking about her students impressed him, too. Rachel hadn't seemed too sure about helping with the fundraiser—until he'd gotten her talking about the children. It was clear they had a lot in common.

It's been a long time since a woman caught my attention, he thought. *I'm letting work take over my life.*

He'd noticed a small spark between them. Only time would tell if it was worth pursuing.

There wasn't time for that now, of course. He could take her for lunch—a proper date, not a business meeting—once the gala was over.

Speaking of lunch and the gala... Scott walked to his desk to gather ideas for the fundraiser's food. It was rare that he had time to brainstorm during his shift. He needed to stop daydreaming and get back to work. Scott was jotting down questions for the caterer when Adam walked behind him and cleared his throat.

"Am I interrupting? The pediatric beds are empty, but we've got an older teenager in the waiting room. Triage is asking if they can use your beds."

Scott closed the folder and nodded. "I was just making notes for the gala. I want the food to remind people we're raising money for kids. Make it kid-friendly, but fancy enough to justify the price of a ticket. Echoes of childhood favorites, like a sophisticated mac and cheese or a chocolate fondue. Everybody loves chocolate, right?"

Adam grinned. "My nephew would eat chocolate for breakfast if we let him. Stop by the Oyster and Pearl and look at their kid's menu," he suggested. "It's the fanciest restaurant in town. They can give you some ideas."

Scott wasn't the only one with a head for planning these things, he thought humbly. Was there anything his nurse wasn't good at?

He turned off any thoughts of Rachel or the gala as he took long strides toward their temporary pediatric unit, using the walk to focus himself. Time to get back to work.

The next few minutes were a rush of activity. The teenager in the lobby had left a small puddle of blood on the floor. Scott shook his head. The adult nurses working triage were still getting used to pediatric staff who could deal with overflow. The boy should have been sent straight back for treatment.

He spent some time making the boy's hand numb and examining the deep, long cut that brought him to the emergency room. While Scott worked, he tried to distract the kid with conversation. "This is impressive. How did this happen, young man?"

"Home ec accident," the teen said, wrinkling his nose. "We were chopping onions. The onion won."

"Well, I'm guessing you drowned that onion in blood and tears. I'd say the knife won this battle." Scott examined the boy's hand, pleased that there was no damage besides the bleeding. The tendons and arteries all looked intact. The kid got lucky—this could have ended badly. Still, hands bled a lot. Wounds like this needed stitches to minimize blood loss and scarring.

Scott held back a sigh as he prepared his suturing kit. He was trained to do stitches. But if he got his wish, they'd have a pediatric plastic surgeon on staff soon.

While Scott's stitches weren't as neat as a surgeon's, he could get the job done and stop the bleeding. "This might leave a scar, but you'll have a fun story to tell. Think of something more exciting than chopping an onion."

The kid grinned as the doctor worked. "Great. Girls like scars."

Scott and Adam both laughed. "That's why I'm still single," Adam said with a grin. "I don't have enough scars."

Instead of grinning at his nurse's joke, Scott chuckled darkly. Every medical staff member gained scars over the years, but none of them were visible. Being an emergency room doctor wasn't great for your mental health. He'd helped lots of kids, but not all of them made it. Losing a patient left deep scars—and not the kind that impressed women.

His mind drifted back to Rachel as he stitched up the boy's hand. She was a friendly young woman. Maybe lunch was a bad idea. She didn't deserve to be connected with someone like him. Work kept him too busy to form lasting relationships, and he had too much damage to become involved with a woman like Rachel.

Scars or no scars, there was a reason most doctors married early in their careers. It was tough to find someone who understood the burden of a full-time physician, without watching that doctor grow into their job.

Scott tugged the last stitch tight and knotted the thread. "What do you think?" He gestured toward the teen's hand, stained yellow with disinfectant and a neat line of stitches running along the cut.

The boy held up his hand it inspect it. "Cool. I can't wait to show the kids at school. Thanks, doc. It doesn't hurt at all."

Scott chuckled and printed out discharge instructions for the boy's parents. "The nerve block will wear off soon. Tylenol should ease the pain when it does. Take it easy for a few days."

The boy's mother nodded and murmured her thanks. Within a few minutes, they were both gone, out of Scott's life and part of a long list of former patients.

Scott walked down the hall, feeling good about a job well done. You could make a real difference with the right training. If only every problem was so easily solved.

Chapter Five

Rachel

RACHEL CHOSE ONE OF the last open seats at Grace Lutheran Church. She'd helped with Kindness Committee projects before, but this was her first time attending a meeting.

People around the table smiled as they glanced her way. Her friends Brook Reed and Avery Danielson were there. She knew a few others from volunteering with the committee, too.

Brad Brown, Brook's boyfriend and Avery's brother, caught her attention by waving his cane. They'd been working together on the town's egg hunt when he broke his ankle. Rachel had driven him to the hospital that day, where she'd met Scott for the first time.

Her stomach fluttered as she thought about meeting Scott for lunch a few days ago.

Calm down, Rachel reminded the butterflies in her tummy. *We're working together, not dating. Keep it professional.*

She distracted herself by continuing to look around the room. Harry Anderson had also helped with the egg hunt, and waved his own cane at her with a wide grin. His cane wasn't because he'd broken his ankle, but because the elderly man was clumsy on his feet. He made up for his lack of agility by having a wicked sense of humor. Harry was a fun guy to be around.

Fun or not, Rachel believed it was time to step up. If she wanted to help the hospital and become involved in the community, the Kindness Committee was the place to be.

Pastor Rick Harris lead the group through an opening prayer, then launched straight into the meeting's agenda. "Our spring food drive was a success. The pantry's shelves are filled with canned goods and boxes! Thank you to everyone who helped." He turned to nod at Avery and Brad. "The Clint Brown Kindness Fund's table was also a big success. We raised enough money to stuff a bookbag for every child in the elementary school this fall. We'll need a committee to purchase the supplies and fill bookbags before the first day of school. Any volunteers?"

"I'm in." Brad raised his hand and nodded at his sister. "Grandpa would like what we're doing in his name."

"I can help, too." Rachel raised her hand and gestured toward the pastor. "I'll find a list of supplies for each grade."

"Excellent idea. Any other helpers?" Pastor Rick jotted down a few more names as people raised their hands.

They walked through the rest of the agenda items before the pastor opened the floor to new discussions.

Rachel raised her hand again. "Are we doing anything for the hospital expansion?"

"Not yet. I heard they're planning a fundraiser, but I don't know a lot of details."

She nodded and opened her folder and notebook. Scott's organization skills were rubbing off on her. "I'm helping with the event. I've recruited twenty-seven students to sing in a children's choir that night. A few of their parents are asking how they can help, too. It might be nice to have the school and kindness committee involved in our own fundraiser."

Rachel swallowed down a sense of unease as she finished talking. A second fundraiser was a good idea, but she was worried about stretching herself too thin. Still, she was in a unique position to help Scott and Pastor Rick work together. If anyone could amplify the hospital's efforts and get kids like Aubrey better medical care, it was the Kindness Committee.

Brook leaned forward, crossing her arms on the table as she looked at Rachel. "What ideas do you have?"

"The hospital is hosting a silent auction with music and dancing. We could have our own auction or basket raffle. Ask the community for donations." Rachel grinned as she glanced through at her notes. "From what I understand, the gala is featuring expensive prizes, like a weekend getaway in Paris. Most parents can't afford a trip to France. They want to win a gift card from our local bookstore, or a dozen cupcakes."

"Emma works at the bookstore. We could ask her for a donation." Brook twisted her lips as she counted out their local businesses. "I can give a gift card to my bakery, and put together some baskets from the local restaurants. The spa is popular, too. Give some lucky mom a chance to win a massage."

"I went to high school with the owner of the dolphin tour company," Brad volunteered. "I can talk him into donating a few hours for a private tour."

Avery raised her hand. "What about a fun run? My daughter did a fun run at her old school, before we moved here. Each kid paid thirty dollars and got a T-shirt. The shirts were donated, so the school kept the registration fee. The kids had a blast and the school raised a lot of money."

"These are all great ideas." Pastor Rick jotted notes onto a whiteboard at the front of the room. "What else can we do?"

Grant Danielson, Avery's husband, sat back in his chair. "We can have the basket raffle during the fun run. People were generous when we put out a jar and asked for donations, too. Tell them why their support matters. Give them a chance to feel like they're involved in the town's progress."

"That makes sense." Harry nodded. "People ask me for money all the time, but they don't help my town or family. My grandkids can use this hospital. I'd throw a few extra dollars in a jar."

Rachel's eyes shimmered with tears as she looked around the table. She was new to the Kindness Committee, but they'd jumped in when she asked for help. Neighbors helped neighbors here. They cared about each other.

They tossed around other ideas. Someone suggested face painting. Brook agreed to organize a bake sale during the run, which started a minor argument with her boyfriend. He ate most of the baked goods when he helped.

"If I make a dozen cookies, you'll eat ten of them," she said, nudging him in the ribs. "Why don't you help with the basket raffle instead?"

"Your baking is too yummy to resist." Brad leaned in for a kiss and smiled. "You'll raise more money than everyone else combined, especially if I'm your official taste-tester. It's a fun symmetry, right? I'm building the hospital. Now you're helping, too." He wrapped his arm around her and gave her a squeeze. "Look at us, working together."

Rachel tried not to stare at her friends' affection. She didn't mind being one of the few single teachers at work. Rachel was too busy to consider dating. But maybe she didn't want to be alone forever.

Her mind wandered toward Scott. She wondered if the single doctor felt lonely too, even with his hectic schedule.

Pastor Rick cleared his throat. "Back on topic. My niece likes to do face painting. Should I call her?"

Rachel pulled herself together and jotted down the newest ideas. Time to focus, no matter how heart-meltingly cute her friends could be. Her next step would be to contact the elementary school principal. They'd need the school board to approve these ideas.

But for now, they had a plan. If she had a say, both fundraisers would be a tremendous success. Even if she had to juggle a handsome doctor and a growing sense of loneliness.

This project was about her kids. There was no room for failure.

Chapter Six

Scott

Scott grinned as he disconnected a call with his business director. Any concerns he'd had about working with Rachel were gone. Not only had she rounded up enough children for a children's choir, but she was also organizing a fun run, basket raffle, and bake sale.

Rachel was still ironing out the details. They had a lot of support already, though—the PTO was ready to help, and the Sunset Cove Kindness Committee was on board.

He'd stumbled on a real blessing when he met Rachel Lancaster.

She'd scheduled the run the week before school ended. That was pretty soon, but Rachel thought they could pull everything together in time. It also meant Rachel could focus on one fundraiser at a time—the gala wasn't until mid-summer.

The two events would pull from a different pool of donors. The gala would attract deep-pocket sponsors from across the region, while Rachel's fun run and basket raffle would bring in the families who would benefit from the hospital expansion.

It was a brilliant way to raise more money for the children's ward.

Today, he'd be walking through the construction site for the new pediatric wing. Rachel was joining him, along with the hospital board and a few of their biggest financial supporters.

Leaving his notes behind, Scott walked down to the hospital entrance to meet the tour guide.

Grant Danielson, the owner of Grant Construction and one of Rachel's friends, was there to greet them. He handed out hard hats after shaking every person's hand. "We're doing a quick walk-through today. It's a chance to see how things are progressing," he said. "We've got virtual tours on the website, but there's nothing like walking through the site."

Grant held open a heavy, fireproof door for the team and gestured for them to enter. William, the hospital's CEO, walked through first. Michelle Newton, one of the board's newest trustees, followed him.

Scott barely knew the woman, but she seemed nice enough. Michelle was a major backer for the expansion project.

She was strikingly tall, with a cascade of blond waves flowing down her back. Not his type. Still, Michelle got a lot of attention when she walked the hospital's halls.

He couldn't help comparing Rachel's understated beauty to Michelle's glamorous appearance. Scott couldn't keep the petite brunette off his mind—and not because of the fundraiser.

He moved to the back of the group, where Rachel hovered uncertainly. His goal today was to make sure Rachel felt comfortable on the tour. If that meant spending more time with her, all the better. "Are you excited?" he asked.

Rachel smiled up at him. "I can't wait. Everyone's eager for the new hospital wing to open. I'm glad they're making progress."

"Let's see how hard Grant is working," he agreed, putting his hand on Rachel's back to guide her through the door.

Scott jumped and removed his hand when he felt a spark. Must be static electricity. Sparks didn't happen in real life. Not because you found a woman attractive. Besides, Scott didn't have the time or mental space for relationships right now. He had a hospital to build.

Still, he refrained from touching Rachel again as he led her toward William and the front of the group. "Have you met our CEO? This is Dr. William Stewart, the head of our hospital. William, this is Rachel Lancaster. She's the teacher organizing our children's choir for the gala."

Rachel held out a hand as they continued down the hallway. "It's nice to meet you, sir. Thanks for allowing me on this tour."

"Couldn't leave you out," William said, pumping her arm up and down. "I've heard good things about you. Sounds like you're working hard to help Scott kick off this fundraiser."

"I'm doing my best. My friends and students are excited to get involved."

William nodded. "That's what I love about this town. Everyone steps up to lend a hand. I couldn't have picked a better place to raise our family." He gave Scott a knowing look. "It's a wonderful town. And we'll make it even better for families once this expansion is done."

Scott cleared his throat. His CEO couldn't know how often Rachel was on Scott's mind. Time to turn the topic away from families before William embarrassed him. "Have either of you seen the new wing yet?"

"I was waiting for the official tour," said William. "We've been talking about this expansion for a decade, and it's finally happening." He turned to Rachel and grinned. "Scott made all of this possible, you know. Our donors were very impressed by his ideas. We couldn't start construction without their support."

"I'm not surprised." Rachel laughed as she looked at Scott. "He was very persuasive when he asked me to join the team."

William nodded. "If your fundraiser is a success, we can move faster than planned. My new goal is to open by the fall. We're grateful to have both of you here to help meet that goal."

Rachel blushed and nodded. "I'm happy to help."

Scott looked at his CEO, humbled. They'd hired him to start the expansion. He just hadn't realized how important this role would be—or how much the people of Sunset Cove would mean to him. "Thank you, sir. We'll get this wing built and staffed as quickly as we can."

Scott flushed with both embarrassment and pride as he stood at Rachel's side. As a doctor, he should know his priorities—patients always came first. There was no time to think about pretty brunettes. He had bigger things to focus on.

They entered a large foyer with windows that stretched toward the ceiling.

Grant gathered the group together, gesturing around the room. "This is our children's emergency waiting area. As you can see, it's almost as large as our existing waiting room. We're doubling the space for people who need emergency care, and dedicating this room to children and their parents. Our town has needed this for a long time."

Scott nodded in agreement. Their current waiting room was busy, even in the off-season. Children often had to sit on the floor, sharing their germs and illnesses with the elderly—and witnessing injuries and situations that a child shouldn't see. Separating the adults and kids was a good idea for multiple reasons.

The new waiting room would also have smaller seats and a play area, with a television dedicated to children's cartoons. His goal was to make his patients comfortable. The hospital was already a scary place. No need to make it worse.

"These are the ER treatment rooms," Grant explained, walking past a dozen empty rooms. "They're shells now, but we're almost done painting. Then the medical supply company can add oxygen supply hookups and all the fixtures you need to examine a sick child. Lastly, we'll install the sliding glass doors, bring in pediatric beds, and finish buttoning up the wing."

Scott glanced around, impressed by the team's progress so far. Building and outfitting a new wing wasn't cheap. They needed a strong summer fundraiser to remain on solid ground. But the hospital's board had been adamant about the need for a children's wing, pushing to start construction before raising all the money they needed. For now, the project was funded by grants and early donations. They'd made a lot of progress on a small budget.

Scott was glad they'd pushed forward. It was a lot easier to raise money once you started a construction project. People wanted progress. They didn't want a virtual tour before writing a check.

Rachel paused outside the steel doors that led to an elevator shaft. "What's upstairs?"

"I can't let you up there yet. Our specialty offices will be on the second floor." Grant pointed toward the ceiling. "They'll treat patients during the day, but they can also be available for emergencies in the ER."

Scott stepped forward and nodded. "Our specialists will do rotations with admitted patients, too. We won't be as advanced as CHOP, of course. But we'll meet a need for the less-complex cases and keep kids closer to home."

He gestured toward the elevator, mirroring Grant's movements. "We'll have a few beds on the third floor for hospitalized kids and slowly expand. The fourth floor will eventually be reserved for chemotherapy patients. These things take time, but we've made exciting progress."

Rachel grinned as Scott pulled her aside, letting the rest of the group pass them. "I'm glad you asked me to help with the gala. You got my email about the school's fun run?"

"I've shared it with a few people at the hospital. You're doing an incredible job. If you need any help with your own fundraiser, let me know."

As they spoke, a lock of hair fell out of Rachel's clip and brushed across her face. Scott reached out to brush it back, then dropped his arm, letting his hand swing awkwardly between them. He held back a groan as the scent of her shampoo drifted toward him.

He needed to leave before he made a fool of himself. "It's my turn to work the overnight shift. I should get back for handover. The tour is almost done, anyway. Are you okay without me?"

"I'll be fine. I'll text you once the school approves our run."

Scott raised his arm again, this time to wave goodbye to Grant. He hustled away from the construction site. Scott didn't stop until he was past the security officer. Once he was past the heavy wooden doors separating the new wing from the rest of the hospital, he took off his construction hat and closed his eyes.

Could he be any more awkward? Scott had no business getting into a relationship with Rachel or anyone else.

His full attention needed to remain on work. His patients needed him.

Chapter Seven

Rachel

RACHEL TAPPED HER FEET as she sat outside the principal's office. She was here to discuss the school's fundraiser with her boss, but sitting in these chairs always made her worry that she'd done something wrong.

She'd moved to Sunset Cove a few years ago, so she'd never attended Sunset Elementary. Still, every principal's office felt the same. They felt like trouble.

Rachel held back a giggle. She was a grown woman and a working professional, and still afraid of the principal's office.

She jumped in her chair as Allen Sawyer, the elementary school principal, came out of his office to greet her. Rachel smoothed out her skirt and attempted to calm her nerves at the same time.

"Good to see you, Rachel. I'm glad you emailed me." The principal held out his hand and gave hers a firm shake. He gestured for her to enter the office, then closed the door behind them. "I hear you're busy raising money for the local hospital. Is that what today's meeting is about?"

Rachel settled into the chair in front of his desk and nodded. "I'm working on the hospital gala, but the Kindness Committee is helping me put on our own event. Most parents won't be able to attend the gala, so we're giving them a chance to support the pediatric wing with a smaller fundraiser."

"What did you have in mind? How can I help?"

"We won't need much help. We just need permission to use the school. So far, we've planned a basket raffle in the gym, a bake sale in the cafeteria, and a one-mile run across the school grounds."

Allen leaned forward and rested his arms on his desk. "Ambitious. You seem passionate about raising money for the hospital."

Rachel nodded. "It was difficult to watch Aubrey go through chemotherapy. Maybe things would have been easier if she stayed closer to home. I'd like to make that possible."

"My nephew met the hospital's new pediatrician last week. He needed stitches after slicing up his hand. My sister said Dr. Hart was nice. Friendly, and put them all at ease."

Rachel smiled. She thought back to the first time she'd met Scott—how he'd made her feel like an important part of his fundraising team. She hadn't seen him work with kids yet, but imagined he was great with both teens and young children.

"We'll have to get this project approved by the school board," he continued. "But I'm happy to support you."

"Thank you, sir. I appreciate it." Rachel resisted doing a little dance, but couldn't help being excited about the principal's support. If he was on their side, the school board would probably approve their proposal.

Rachel pulled her attention back to the principal. To her surprise, he was sitting back in his chair with his arms folded, watching her closely. "Rachel, we've known each other a long time." He leaned forward and looked her in the eyes. "I'm concerned about you. Are you stretching yourself too thin? You've got a lot on your plate already."

She twisted her lips into a wry smile and nodded. "I can't do this alone, so I've got a few friends helping. My friend Brook owns Seaside Cupcakes. She's in charge of the bake sale. The Kindness Committee is taking over the basket raffle. I'll organize the run."

"Will you have enough time for that?"

Rachel nodded. "I can handle it. The run is the weekend before school ends. I've got the entire summer to relax."

Her boss looked at her with concern. "Delegate some tasks to other people. Don't take on too much work. But you're right, things will be easier once summer starts. Just a few more weeks," he assured her. "The end of the school year is always hard."

Rachel left the office feeling confident that she'd made the right choice. There were a lot of parents pushing for a smaller fundraiser. If the Kindness Committee could pull this off, they'd help bring better medical care to her students.

And as she'd told her principal, she had the entire summer to recover from a busy year. Rachel had promised to help Brook in the bakery this summer, but she was looking forward to spending time with her friend. A few hours of baking and selling cupcakes was nothing compared to her current schedule.

Rachel practically skipped to her classroom, pleased that everything was coming together. She had choir practice after school today. She'd finalize their song list this week, and meet with Scott soon to have the list approved.

Her stomach fluttered as she thought about meeting the handsome doctor again. Rachel pushed those thoughts aside. No time to worry about handsome Scott. They were two professionals, working together.

Time to prepare for choir rehearsal.

Rachel's jaw dropped as the children in her music room began to sing.

It was only their second rehearsal. All the students had permission to take part in the hospital fundraiser. They'd meet after school each week. There wasn't much time to work together, but their excitement made up for their lack of rehearsal time.

She'd sent two songs home with the students last week, and it sounded like each of them had practiced until they were nearly perfect.

Rachel clapped her hands as the song ended. She hit the "pause" button on her music player. "Boys and girls, that was wonderful! Who practiced this song at home?" She grinned as every hand shot into the air. "If you keep practicing, this is going to be a great performance."

She shook her head in amazement and looked down at the music stacked on top of her piano. Rachel hadn't planned to feature any children in solos, but there was a lot more talent here than she'd realized. She shuffled through the music she'd gathered from the middle school choir director.

Rachel picked out a song from the middle of the stack and studied it. Were her kids capable of more difficult music? She'd need Scott to approve their list of songs, but first, she needed to know what the kids could handle. "Does anyone want to sing alone? In a solo?" She grinned as ten hands flew into the air. "You can each take a turn showing me what you practiced this week. One verse each."

She grabbed a notebook and jotted down notes as each student sang. These kids were very talented. Nothing she'd be ashamed to feature, even at a fancy gala like Scott was planning.

But when Emily Wilde sang, Rachel knew she had found their soloist. Rachel's arms erupted in goosebumps as the young girl sang a beautiful melody, full of soul and deep with emotion.

"Emily, that was beautiful!" Rachel struggled to conceal her grin as Emily sat back down, but she did her best. It was important to treat each of the students equally. Not to show favorites. "Who else wants to sing for me?"

She continued to take notes while two more boys and one girl sang alone. More than ever, Rachel was confident they could put together a good show.

Her optimism grew as the children walked out the door and into the hallway. This program would be hard work, but it would be worth it. They'd raise a lot of money for the hospital and create new ties between the school and the community.

She didn't bother holding back her grin as she walked students to the front door.

Before long, nearly every parent had picked up their child. Emily stood alone in front of the school.

The girl stared at the sidewalk, tracing an invisible pattern on top of the concrete. "Sometimes my dad is late," she mumbled. "I'm sorry. He forgets when it's his turn. My mom and dad don't live together."

Rachel kneeled down to Emily's level and smiled at her. "It's no problem. Let's sit on the bench together." The two of them sat down, watching cars drive past the school and enjoying the warm spring breeze. "What did you think about choir practice?"

A smile lit up Emily's face. "It was a lot of fun. I hope you do it again next year."

Rachel hesitated. The choir was supposed to be a one-time thing for the hospital fundraiser. She already had a full schedule with classes and recorder concerts. Could she take on a children's choir next year, too?

As much as her brain shouted *no*, a picture formed inside her head. Rachel imagined students gathered at Christmas time, putting on a concert for their families. Fifth graders singing at their moving-up ceremony, a final farewell before they went to middle school. Teaching children to love singing. This was a type of music they could continue throughout their lives, even without lessons or an instrument.

"I hadn't considered having a choir next year, but it might be a good idea," she admitted. "We'll see what happens."

The two grinned at each other. Just then, a red sports car screeched to a halt in front of the school.

Emily jumped to her feet. "My dad's here. You should stay on the bench," she muttered. "He can be strange around some people."

Rachel frowned, but stood up anyway. It was her job to see kids safely into their parents' care. She'd hand Emily off to her dad, then go inside to lock up her classroom.

She nodded as the man approached both of them, then held out her hand. "You must be Emily's dad. I'm Ms. Lancaster, the music teacher. Thanks for picking her up after choir practice."

To Rachel's surprise, he gripped her hand firmly and tugged her closer. "Hello, Ms. Lancaster. My name's Cory. I didn't realize Emily had such a pretty music teacher."

The words were innocent enough, even if they were a little too flirtatious for her taste. But there was something about the way Cory looked at her. She shuddered and tried to tug her hand out of his grasp. He held firm.

Rachel frowned and pulled harder. "Thanks for the compliment, but I need to get going," she said.

She gave her hand a final yank. But once her hand was free, he reached for her arm.

"Why the rush? I'll drop Emily off at her mom's house. We can get a drink at the bar. My place is close by. How does that sound?" he asked, smoothly rubbing his hand over her arm.

Words failed Rachel as she stared at Cory. Was he really suggesting they dump his daughter and go drinking? She glanced down at Emily, but the girl wasn't looking at her. Emily stared at the ground as if this happened all the time.

Rachel felt a rush of relief as the school door opened and Allen Sawyer strode toward them. "Good evening, Ms. Lancaster. Hello, sir." He nodded toward Emily's father. "I'm sorry to interrupt, but I need you inside. I've got a few questions about the basket raffle."

Rachel nodded and yanked her arm free from Cory's grasp. "I'm coming. Wait for me, please. Will you be okay, Emily?" She forced a smile onto her face, trying not to show how concerned she was.

When Emily gave her a glum nod, Rachel walked back into the building with her boss. She let out a sigh of relief as the doors locked behind them.

Allen kept a smile on his face as they walked into the school. He turned to face Rachel once they were in his office. "Are you okay? It looked like you needed help."

She collapsed into a chair and shuddered. "I'm fine, but thanks for stepping in. Mr. Wilde asked me to come home with him. He wouldn't let go of my arm." Rachel closed her eyes and tried not to cry. "What kind of dad propositions a woman in front of his child? I thought he would drag me into his car."

The principal nodded and opened the emergency contact file on his computer. "I'm calling Emily's mother right now. She should know what happened. This is a safe community, but we work hard to keep it that way. I'll be outside after every choir rehearsal now. Don't walk outside by yourself again. Understood?"

Rachel nodded numbly, still trying to process what had happened. She'd grown up in Michigan, in a city with one of the highest crime rates in America. Women walked to their cars in groups there.

People could walk alone in Sunset Cove. She'd never expected something like this to happen in their beachside town.

She sat listening to her boss call Emily's mother, then jumped when her phone vibrated with an incoming text.

Scott

> Are you free in an hour? The gala's hotel is giving me a tour.

Rachel stared at her phone. While she was falling apart, the world continued to turn. Rachel held her head higher. Nothing had happened outside. She was safe. And for some reason, she knew Scott would keep her safe. He'd never let someone like Cory hurt her.

The thought was oddly comforting.

> Give me the address. I'll meet you there.

Chapter Eight

Scott

SCOTT PULLED INTO THE Golden Tides parking lot as Rachel was getting out of her car. Perfect timing.

He grinned. He'd been in a better mood since texting Rachel.

Scott wasn't looking for a relationship, but he enjoyed spending time with Rachel. Something about her made Scott smile—and he still barely knew her.

He parked his Jeep next to Rachel's car and waved through the open window. "Thanks for coming. It's my first chance to see the ballroom. I thought you'd want to be here, too."

Rachel sized up the imposing hotel, her eyes widening at the flawless landscaping and Victorian columns gracing the front entrance. "I've only lived in Sunset Cove for a few years. I haven't been inside the Golden Tides yet. It's a bit outside my price range."

Scott nodded as they walked through the parking lot. He put his hand on the small of her back and guided her through the door. "You need an impressive space to attract generous donors. Plus, the owner's a supporter of the hospital. He's donating the ballroom for the night."

The owner's generosity still surprised Scott. He wasn't used to small-town life. People took care of each other here.

Scott had worked in a lot of big cities during his training, and enjoyed knowing that entertainment and good food were just a few blocks away. You couldn't say that about Sunset Cove. There were still some perks to small-town living.

More and more, he thought Sunset Cove could become home. It might even be a good place to start a family.

The idea stopped him cold. Where had that come from? Having a family was out of his reach. He was too busy, and didn't have time to dedicate to kids or a wife. It wasn't fair for someone else to live with his hectic schedule.

But would his life be hectic forever? Once they hired more pediatric staff, he'd have more flexibility. Less time on call.

Rachel turned to him and frowned. Scott jumped, realizing that he'd frozen in place. His hand was still touching her back.

Keep it together, he thought. *Get through the gala. Then we'll see where life takes you.*

"Everything okay?" she asked.

"Just thinking." He smiled and continued moving forward, bringing her with him.

Rachel went willingly. "I'm sure you've got a lot on your mind. This fundraiser is a big deal. The community's been waiting for the hospital's expansion for months. It's all the parents can talk about."

"I'm glad the parents are excited. It makes the long hours more bearable." Scott smiled down at Rachel as he guided her through the hotel foyer. He pulled open the heavy doors that led to the ballroom. "We're meeting the event coordinator today. She wanted to show us the space before we formalize our plans."

His eyes swept through the space, from the glamorously treated windows to the towering ceiling. The enormous room was beautiful, elegant, and perfect for the gala. Scott grinned at Rachel, pleased. He hadn't known a place like this existed in Sunset Cove.

"Welcome!" The event coordinator entered the room and opened her arms wide to give Scott a hug. She did the same for

Rachel, leaning in for a kiss on each cheek. "Welcome to Golden Tides. My name is Maria Russo, and I'm the director of onsite events. I'm glad you could make it today."

Maria walked them around the room, pointing out the best areas for dancing, food, and musicians. "How many people do you expect?"

"We've sold over a hundred tickets, but were hoping for more as we ramp up advertising," Scott said.

"That's perfect. We have space for three hundred, especially if the weather cooperates. Let me show you the outdoor courtyard."

They stood outside, discussing the logistics of summer weather and indoor-outdoor events for a few minutes, before returning to the main room.

This space is perfect, he thought. Scott glanced at Rachel again, hoping to see a similar expression of delight on her face—but she didn't look excited by the room's elegance. Instead, she looked slightly confused.

Scott leaned closer to speak to her, hesitating as he gauged her reaction. "It's a great space, isn't it?"

"It's beautiful. Very elegant." Rachel stared at the inlaid tile floor, refusing to meet his eyes. "A lot fancier than I expected, though."

Scott's brow furrowed. What had she been expecting? This was a huge fundraiser, with important supporters.

"It's a perfect place for your gala," Maria chimed in. "We held a similar event here last year."

Scott nodded in agreement, wishing that Maria would let him handle this. Rachel looked greener by the minute—and he needed to find out why. "When people pay five hundred dollars a head, they expect a location like this. I hadn't expected to find a suitable space so close to the hospital. Sunset Cove isn't a high-end beach town. This is like a hidden gem."

"Golden Tides attracts the higher-end clientele on this side of town. Private getaways, business functions, things like that. We are designed to impress." Maria smiled demurely, gesturing toward the room.

But Rachel still didn't look happy. Instead, she stared up at the delicate chandeliers suspended from the ceiling. A look of shock filled her face. "Five hundred dollars. For dinner. And you want my students to entertain them. Are you sure about this?" she hissed. "I've had a tough day. Don't play games with me."

Scott stared at her with surprise. They needed to attract people willing to open their wallets and donate generously. That was one reason he liked the school's fun run and basket raffle—bring the community together for a smaller event, and attract the big spenders with a gala and silent auction.

"This isn't a game. The fundraising board approved the location," he assured her quietly. "Let's talk about this outside. But yes, I still think having your students sing is a great idea. Let's finish the tour, then we'll chat."

Maria took a few more notes as Scott showed where the hors d'oeuvres stations should begin. She also asked Rachel a few questions about the choir. "How many children are performing?"

"About thirty kids, give or take a few," Rachel stuttered. "All in fourth and fifth grade. We've had a few more children join."

Maria smiled, noted the number of performers, and closed her folder. She held her hand out to give Scott and Rachel a firm handshake. "That's all I need. I'll have space prepared for the choir, the string quartet, and the food. Spend as much time here as you'd like. Familiarize yourself with the room." She held out a business card for each of them. "Call me if you have questions."

Once they were alone again outside, Rachel whirled toward Scott. She didn't bother to keep her voice down this time. "You're selling tickets for five hundred dollars each, and you want my students to sing to them? They're not professionals. They'll be booed off the stage." Her shoulders shrugged in defeat. "I want to help you, but I can't do this to my kids. It's not fair."

Scott shook his head. He respected that she looked out for her students. Scott guarded his patients fiercely, too. Their lives were private, and the details of their medical care should stay private, too—unless they volunteered to share their story. "You're not the only entertainment. We've got a string quartet to provide music for most of the night. We just want to showcase some kids from town. People love seeing how their generosity can benefit the community."

Rachel just shook her head. "I still think you're crazy."

"I'll be as crazy as it takes to get this hospital built," he chuckled. "Trust me. We've thought this through. Your students belong here. Now, what about that song list? You had a preliminary list of songs you'd perform at the gala."

Rachel reached into her purse and pulled out a slightly wrinkled piece of paper, handing it to him with shaking hands. "It's a mix of pop culture songs and show tunes. They go over well with larger crowds. But if we're performing here, I should rethink our plans."

But Scott scanned over the paper with a grin. "These songs are perfect. They're upbeat and positive. You're on the right track."

Rachel hesitated, then nodded. "I'll talk to you soon," she said, backing away and quickly climbing into her car.

Scott watched her with concern. Would Rachel stick with the fundraiser? Or would she call tomorrow, full of apologies and telling Scott she no longer wanted to be involved?

Having kids perform was a good idea. But to his surprise, he realized that working with Rachel was even more important. He enjoyed their time together. It was nice having an excuse to call or text her.

Scott tapped the song list against his steering wheel and grinned. Wasn't life funny? He'd stumbled onto a woman with a schedule as crazy as his, and he couldn't get her off his mind.

Now he prayed she wouldn't walk away.

Chapter Nine

Rachel

RACHEL DRUMMED HER HANDS on her steering wheel, furious that she'd fallen for Scott's idea. He was setting them both up for embarrassment. Sure, her students were great. They were learning to work together as a choir. But they weren't good enough for a fundraiser charging *five hundred dollars per ticket*.

She needed backup—friends who could be there when she pulled out of the fundraiser. They'd do the fun run and basket raffle. Earn a few dollars for the hospital. That would have to be enough. It was better to back out now, before they made fools of themselves.

Rachel grabbed her phone and pulled up her friends' latest group message.

> Emergency meeting at Seaside Cupcakes. Who's in?

Rachel's panic drained away as her friends replied.

Brook
> Back door is open.

Avery
> Grant will watch the kids. See you soon.

Emma
> Dropping my kid at Avery's, then headed your way.

Kerry
> Be there in 20.

Rachel covered her mouth and began to cry. What would she do without her friends? They dropped everything in a heartbeat, just for her. She sent up another prayer of thanks for her amazing friends. Rachel didn't have any family in Sunset Cove—but who needed family when you had these four women in your corner?

She parked in front of Seaside Cupcakes a few minutes later. Time to pull herself together. Even the best friends in the world couldn't help her if she was a blubbering, incoherent mess.

Rachel took a deep breath and walked through the bakery's door. Four concerned faces and a plate of chocolate chip cookies greeted her.

A single tear fell down her face as she looked at each of her friends. "Thanks for coming. I need some help."

"And a hug, too?" Emma pushed herself away from the kitchen counter and wrapped her arms around Rachel. "Emergency meetings call for hugs."

Rachel let herself relax in her friend's arms. Yes, she needed a hug. They'd talk things over. Her friends would back her up. And at least she'd have company when she torpedoed Scott's fundraising plans.

She felt horrible backing out at this point. Scott was advertising the children's choir as part of the night's entertainment. They'd had a few more students join the choir—including Aubrey O'Grady, the girl who went through chemotherapy at CHOP. Aubrey had volunteered to talk to the crowd after the choir performed.

The thought sent shivers down Rachel's spine. She'd heard Aubrey talk about overcoming cancer. The young girl told a powerful story. If Aubrey talked to the crowd, she would soften even the hardest hearts and encourage more donations.

Not that any of this mattered. Sure, Scott was telling people to expect a children's choir. But if they were paying five hundred dollars a ticket, they expected something fancier than thirty kids from Sunset Cove Elementary School. She was saving Scott and her students a lot of embarrassment by dropping out.

Rachel gave Emma one last squeeze, then gestured toward the dining area. "Should we get more comfortable? Let's go find a booth."

Emma nodded and grabbed the cookies. Brook followed them through the door, then stood behind the cafe counter. "Is this a coffee meeting? Smoothies? Or should I find something with more kick in my apartment upstairs?"

"Let's save the kick for later. Coffee works." Rachel felt another surge of appreciation for her friends. "Thanks for coming today. I have to drop out of the hospital fundraiser, and I need your help telling Scott."

"What?!" Brook exclaimed, rushing around the counter to face Rachel. "You worked so hard on the children's choir. The kids are doing great. Did something happen?"

"The Golden Tides happened," Rachel said wryly. "It's this expensive hotel on the outskirts of town. Scott wants to charge a thousand dollars per couple for the gala. My students can't perform for these people. They're expecting professional musicians. There's going to be a *string quartet* performing before us. We'll sound horrible next to them."

Avery shook her head, watching Rachel carefully. "You're one of the most talented women I know. If anyone can do this, it's you. Besides, people are donating money for a children's hospital. They probably like children. They'll be okay if the string quartet stops to let the kids sing."

Brook brought a tray of drinks to the table. "Four iced coffees, and one smoothie for the pregnant mama," she said, smiling down at Avery. "So we've established that your students *can* perform at a fancy fundraiser. Scott thinks it's a good idea. Why do you want to back out?"

"I'm scared," Rachel admitted, the truth making her face flush with shame. "Sure, I'm scared that the kids will be embarrassed. The further we go with this fundraiser, the more I realize that it's a big deal. I'm scared to mess it up by picking the wrong songs, or letting the wrong kid sing a solo. This is too important. I'm not good enough to be in charge."

"Kendra says you taught the fourth grade class to play the alma mater on recorder," Emma said quietly. "They'll be playing for the elementary school graduation. You tell kids they can do big, important things. What will they learn if you drop out of the gala? They'll think they're not good enough. That's not a lesson you want them to learn."

A knot formed in Rachel's stomach as she considered Emma's words. This would be a horrible lesson to teach her students. She was always telling them to keep trying. Never to give up.

And here she was, giving up.

Rachel put her head on the table and groaned. Her friends were right. She'd have to bump up their performance to something more special, but she couldn't just quit the gala.

Brook pushed aside her icy drink and wrapped an arm around Rachel's shoulders. "Now tell us what's going on. Hot doctor giving you trouble? This isn't like you. You've never backed down from a challenge before."

Despite her mood, Rachel chuckled. "He's a hot doctor, but he's not interested in me. We're both too busy to date right now. When he's not working in the emergency room, he's planning this fundraiser."

"So have a working date. Get together, enjoy some food, and talk about the hospital. Lots of busy couples make their schedules work. Brad brings his work to the bakery, and works while I bake." Brook gave Rachel another squeeze, then pulled her arm back and gave her shoulder a nudge. "It's been a long time since you've been on a date."

Rachel shook her head. "There's no time. Unless I date someone at the elementary school, there's no way I'd see a boyfriend. My days and nights are filled right now. I'm not even supposed to be alone, so it's not like I can sneak away for a lunch date, either..." Rachel's voice trailed off.

Not a topic I planned to bring up, she thought, picking up her drink with a shaking hand. "This is the best iced coffee I've ever had. Did you get a new machine?"

"Nope, same old coffee machine. Why aren't you supposed to be alone?" Brook asked, mirroring Rachel's attempt at casualness.

Rachel silently cursed her friend's observation skills. She sighed and set her drink back down. "It's nothing. There was a dad at pickup, after choir practice. He got pretty intense and tried to get me into his car."

"Whoa, that's crazy. I know parents worry about kidnapping, but to get a teacher in your car? That takes nerve." Emma shook her head. "I thought we were safe in a small town."

Rachel shuddered as the scene played through her mind again. "He had his hand around my arm. The principal said I shouldn't be alone outside the school."

"When did this happen?" Brook raised her eyebrows. "You should have told us sooner. We're all busy, but we could take turns being your buddy. I agree with the principal. You shouldn't be alone."

Rachel chewed on her lip, wondering how angry her friends would be if she'd kept her problem a secret. She'd never worried about something like this before, even in the city. "It happened today. It's not a big deal. I've just got to be aware of my surroundings and avoid him."

Avery slammed her hand on the table. "It's a huge deal. I'll tell Sophia not to ride the bus for a few days. I'm picking you both up from school and driving you home. What if this creep followed you and found out where you live?"

Rachel's pulse sped up. Was Cory Wilde the type to stalk a teacher? She wasn't sure.

Hopefully Avery was overreacting, but Rachel was grateful for the offer. She had amazing friends.

Those warm and fuzzy feelings disappeared the moment Brook leaned forward. "Creepy dad is taken care of. I'm sure he didn't help your confidence levels when you considered quitting the gala, but we all know your kids will do great. Let's focus on the real problem: Dr. Hot Scott."

Emma snorted and nearly shot iced coffee across the table. "Hot Scott. That's a good one. But look, you're upsetting her." She nodded toward Rachel, who was turning a bright shade of red. "Don't let Brook get to you. She's just teasing."

Rachel huffed out a breath and frowned, wishing that she didn't blush so easily. "I told you, he's not interested in dating. I'm not interested, either. We're two busy professionals working together.

That doesn't mean we're going to fall in love." She glanced down at her almost-empty coffee mug and sighed. "I shouldn't have more caffeine, either. Between the four of you and this coffee, I'm all riled up."

Brook laughed and took their mugs. She set them on the counter, then perched on a stool as she talked to Rachel. "Maybe he's not interested. Maybe he is. You both deserve to have a life outside your jobs. Hard work is important, but so is having fun. There's no point to life if you can't have fun."

Rachel looked pointedly at each of her friends, then rolled her eyes. "I have a life outside of work. See? Having loads of fun here."

Emma reached over and squeezed her hand. "We love spending time with you, and I know it's hard to hear this. We've both been single for too long. It's time to stop making excuses and get out there again."

Chapter Ten

Scott

Scott nodded to the security guard in front of the construction site. "Grant told you I was coming?"

The guard handed him a security badge and hard hat. "Yep. You're on the list. Grant should be here soon."

Scott glanced down the hallway and toward the new foyer. Things were taking shape. The walls were painted and most of the floor was in place. It was a huge step forward from their last tour.

He had the man striding toward him to thank. Grant Danielson wasn't just the owner of Grant Construction—he'd taken on multiple construction teams, coordinating their efforts on the site. He was fast and efficient, and Scott was grateful to have him in charge.

"Welcome back," Grant said, reaching out to shake Scott's hand. "We've made some progress since you visited."

"You got a lot done in two weeks." Scott shook his head as they walked into the nearly-finished foyer. "You're doing a great job. We can't get this project done soon enough, though. I can't believe this town's gone so long without a pediatric unit."

"We made do. I needed plenty of stitches as a kid. Dr. Smith patched me up." Grant held up his arm to show a neat scar. "I'm glad we're doing better for today's kids, though."

Scott held back a sigh of relief. More than one local person had complained the town didn't need a pediatric wing at the hospital.

Change was hard, especially for a small town. Progress could be a scary thing.

But the kids in this town deserved access to pediatricians. That wasn't criticizing the skills of their oldest practicing doctor, who'd worked on Grant and the rest of the town for a generation.

"When we know better, we do better." Scott leaned against the desk that would become the registration hub for families coming into the emergency room. "Kids aren't just miniature adults. The town has grown a lot since you were a kid, too. During tourist season, I'm told your waiting room is overflowing with sick and injured people. A pediatric unit will help kids get care more quickly. In an emergency, minutes and seconds count. Not to mention, no one wants to wait longer than necessary."

Grant nodded, tugging at his construction hat. "I've got a kid coming. My wife Avery's due around Halloween. It's one reason I've pushed the team so hard. I want this wing open before my daughter's born."

Grant Danielson was the perfect man for this job, Scott realized. He had motivation and a hard deadline. Nothing like a growing family to keep you on task. "Congrats, dad."

"Thanks. Lots of things to be excited about." Grant took off his hat and ran a hand through his hair. "Lots of nerves, too. I've always wanted to be a dad. Now I'll have two little girls. One in first grade, and another on the way." He plunked the hat back on his head and grinned, a proud smile lighting up his entire face. "Let's get you back to the exam rooms. I'll show you around before we go back to work. We're on a tight schedule."

What a difference, Scott thought, looking at Grant's progress. The exam rooms didn't have beds or sliding glass doors yet, but they were outfitted with brackets that would hold the vitals monitor, oxygen source, and more. Things had come together quickly, and it was only June. They would be open before fall if the team kept up this pace.

Scott nodded at another construction worker in the hall, then turned his attention to the next exam room. This room was smaller and sky blue. Ceiling tiles mimicked a cloudy day. He'd picked out the ocean-themed decor that would go on the walls—an obvious choice for a seaside hospital.

Yes, this room would be perfect for his young patients. Calming, pleasant, and as un-scary as possible.

Grant pulled his attention from the room by clearing his throat. "Scott? I'd like to introduce you to my lead foreman, Nick Butler. He's been my right-hand man throughout this project."

Scott turned toward Nick with a pleasant smile. Any man who helped Grant accomplish this job quickly was in his good graces. "Pleasure to meet you, Nick. Grant's had you working hard."

Nick threw his head back and laughed. "He's on a mission. First-time dad wants the hospital done as quickly as possible. My wife's just as eager to get the pediatric wing open. We all know this project is important."

"I'm glad we can agree on that. I'll be happy when I'm not working out of the main ER. But it's the kids that will benefit."

Nick nodded. "We're fortunate that our kids are healthy. Not everyone in town has been so lucky. Do you have children?"

Scott held back a sigh. People assumed that if you worked in pediatrics, you must enjoy children and have a few of your own.

Sure, he liked kids. At this point, he'd expected to have a wife and at least one or two kids, plus a dog. Life had gotten in the way.

"No kids," Scott said, trying to keep his tone light. "I'm waiting to meet the right woman."

Nick brightened. "I can fix that. I'm the town's matchmaker."

"Nick..." Grant warned.

"It's true! I matched Grant and his wife. Helped Brook and her boyfriend, too. It's a gift," he said smugly, crossing his arms. "Give me enough time, and I'm sure I could find a match for you in Sunset Cove. Unless you've got your eyes on someone already."

Scott choked back a laugh. Did he have a woman in mind?

He expected his mind to go blank, as it always did when he thought about dating. Instead, a petite music teacher floated to the front of his mind.

Why was Rachel constantly on his mind? That wasn't something to share with the town matchmaker. "No one comes to mind. I spend too much time inside the hospital."

"Not a problem. Just let me…"

"Nick, let's get back to work." Grant shook Scott's hand a final time and walked away. "Leave the guy alone," he called over his shoulder.

Nick grinned and shook his head. "You're working with Rachel this summer, right? She has my number. Call me if you need advice."

That could be awkward, he thought. *Not sure I want to tell Rachel I'm working with a matchmaker.* "Thanks," he said, eager to finish this conversation. "I'll call if I need your help."

Scott shook his head as Nick walked away. He took one last glance around the site, then headed back to his own job.

Funny how one conversation could burn an idea into your brain. He thought about Grant's grin as the man had talked about his daughters. Scott loved kids. But with his workload, who would have patience to start a family with him—let alone put up with a sporadic dating schedule?

A slightly scattered, equally busy teacher popped into his mind again.

He shoved aside any thoughts of Rachel. They needed to keep their relationship professional. No time for fun or dating until after the gala. Maybe not even then. He had a hospital wing to build, and staff to hire.

There was no time to think about pretty brunettes.

Chapter Eleven

Rachel

RACHEL HELD ONTO THE seat in front of her as the school bus rolled down a bumpy road.

It was field trip season, and the fourth graders were headed to the zoo. Rachel had agreed to step in as a last-minute chaperone. She loved spending time with her students—especially the older kids, who would leave for middle school soon.

As if the students in her seat could read her mind, Jude Fischer smiled up at her. "One more year, Ms. Lancaster! One more year until middle school."

"Are you excited?" Rachel said, grinning at her student. "Middle school is a big deal, but you're almost ready."

Jude leaned forward in his seat. "I'm so ready. For summer break, too." He leaned back and smiled. "Only seven days until freedom."

Rachel held back a smile. It had been a long year for everyone, but she wouldn't think about that today. She was going to enjoy her time at the zoo. These kids were ready for summer break—if she was honest, most of the teachers were, too—and they deserved a day away from the classroom.

That's why she joined the kids in cheering when the bus pulled into the zoo's winding entrance road.

The county zoo was a popular destination for most schools in the area. It wasn't too far away. There were lots of animals to look at, which made it educational. And most importantly, it was free. The PTO only had to pay for transportation.

"Settle down, boys and girls," the bus driver called. "We're almost there. Stay in your seats and we'll all get to the zoo safely."

Charlie Campbell had been a bus driver in Sunset Cove for longer than most teachers could remember. He was a real sweetheart. Charlie greeted every kid with a smile and knew most of their names.

As they got off the bus, children swarmed around Rachel.

"Ms. Lancaster, will you be my chaperone?" Emily asked, smiling sweetly.

"Me too! I wanna be in your group!" Jude chimed in.

"You can take all the choir members! It's only fair," another boy added.

Rachel chuckled. Kids had a fun sense of fairness. If Rachel had the energy, she'd chaperone every one of these kids. But there were too many students, and only one of her. "It's up to your teacher. She's got the chaperone list." Rachel pointed toward the head teacher. "Why don't we listen to her? Maybe some of you will be with me."

After a few minutes of commotion, the students settled into their groups and got ready to walk around the zoo. Rachel was pleased to have a group filled with choir kids. To be fair, there were so many fourth graders in choir that the odds had been high.

"I want to see the otters first," Emily said. "They're a lot of fun."

Jude wanted to visit the reptile center. "We need to see the snakes! I love snakes. They'll squeeze you to death if they're hungry. Can we eat a snack there?"

"Sometimes I pretend to be a snake and squeeze my hamburger before I eat it," one of his friends added. "It's more fun to eat that way. That's why snakes like to squeeze their food."

Rachel chucked to herself when the girls in her group squealed in disgust. Pre-teen boys could be a challenge, but they were mostly harmless. Let them get their energy out. Then they'd be ready to listen and learn.

She let her group wander around the reptile house for a few minutes; the students stared at animals while she stood back and took pictures for the yearbook. Once the kids started acting bored and tapping on the animal's enclosures, it was time to move on.

"Team Lancaster, let's go! Your teacher told us to visit the kangaroos. The babies are out of their pouches."

"Cool!" Jude raced for the doorway.

Rachel threw out her arm to stop him. "Take it easy. Those kangaroos took months to grow. They'll still be there if we walk."

As they walked, Rachel's mind wandered toward her schedule for the rest of this week. She had choir practice tonight. Brook was meeting her afterward to make sure she got home safely. She had the best friends.

Rachel was also meeting Scott tomorrow to discuss their plans for the gala. Everything was moving along smoothly now. Yes, the children's choir was new. They weren't professionals. But that's what made it exciting. These kids were working together to help other kids. If they all tried their best, it would be a good night.

Things had worked out with Scott, too. They emailed or talked on the phone every few days, sharing updates and finalizing details. The gala was only six weeks away.

Rachel felt a stab of sadness when she thought about wrapping up the fundraiser. She wouldn't have a reason to talk to Scott anymore. Just like her oldest students were getting ready to move on, she would soon part ways with her new doctor friend.

He was certainly attractive. There was no denying that. He had flirted with her once or twice, too. No one had flirted with her in a long time.

Rachel shook her head. A relationship between them couldn't go anywhere. They both worked long hours. He was always on call, and she spent her nights grading tests and coming up with new lesson plans.

Rachel wouldn't even have a summer break. She was working at the bakery this year. Brook's business was booming, and she couldn't keep up without more help during tourist season.

It's a shame things can't work out with Scott, she thought. *We might make a good couple.*

She thought back to Brook's words about having a life outside work. Sure, she deserved that. But what about reality? Scott was too busy right now. She was, too. They both deserved a partner who could commit time and energy to their relationship.

Rachel had neither time or energy. Her students came first, with the hospital fundraiser a close second.

They reached the kangaroo enclosure, where five little joeys hopped around. The baby kangaroos stayed close to their mothers, ready to jump inside their pouch when they got hungry or scared.

"They're so cute," Emily said. "I love babies."

"Babies are the best." Isaac Forte nodded. "My parents had a baby last month." He turned toward his teacher. "Ms. Lancaster, did you ever have a baby?"

Rachel's heart gave a painful squeeze. It wasn't the first time a student had asked that question. Teachers were supposed to like kids, right? In theory, that meant they should have children.

While most of her co-workers had families, not all of them were so lucky. "No, I've never had a baby. But I have a few hundred children—my students!"

"We don't count," Isaac insisted. "Do you want a baby?"

Rachel hesitated, choosing her words carefully. These were just kids, after all. She watched the kangaroos follow their babies, her heart melting when one joey snuggled against its mother before climbing into its pouch. "Well, I don't want a baby kangaroo," she teased. "They seem like a lot of work. I'm not sure I could make a pouch that would fit a joey."

"My brother poops a lot." Isaac nodded his head, agreeing with Rachel. "He throws up, too. You're making a wise choice."

Rachel swallowed the lump in her throat as her group drifted closer to the kangaroo enclosure. Would she ever have time to commit to a child, or even a boyfriend? Most of her teacher friends were married with school-age children, but Rachel didn't know how they juggled it all.

Avery's baby bump was showing, too. This was her second child—Avery also had an older daughter that Grant was adopting. While she was happy for her friend, Avery's growing family was another reminder that Rachel was still alone.

But she wasn't alone, was she? Rachel had her friends and loved playing with their children. She had a few hundred students to teach and enjoy.

It was only at night, when she returned to her empty apartment, that Rachel felt alone. But what were a few hours of solitude? She spent all day with her favorite young people.

Rachel tried to keep a cheerful face for her students. She pasted on a smile as they fed the giraffes. Kept up a fun conversation on what animals ate during lunch. She even tried to enjoy herself when it was their turn to visit the petting zoo, which was filled with baby goats, cows, and chickens.

She might not have her own family, but these students were like family. Rachel saw most of them for more hours than their parents. Didn't that make her lucky? She didn't have a child, but she touched the lives of countless children each year.

She gave Charlie a tired smile when they got back on the bus. "Ready to drive home?" she asked.

"I'm not feeling so great." The bus driver flinched and rotated his right arm. "The arm's a little sore. Must have slept on it wrong. But I'll get you home."

Rachel sat a few rows behind Charlie. Worry for the driver overrode any sadness about her own life. His skin was pale. She hoped he would be okay.

"How was your group?" one of the parent chaperones asked, clutching an iced coffee from the zoo's food trucks. "My kids tried to climb into the monkey cage. Then they went wild in the gift shop. I had to threaten a time-out."

Rachel glanced back at the dad's group and grimaced. He'd been given some of the rowdiest students in the grade, including his own child. Rachel had been lucky—she'd had a well-behaved group of kids, even if they did tug a few heart-strings.

"Ms. Lancaster, how long until we're home?" Jude asked.

"About thirty minutes. Not too long."

"That's a whole YouTube video!" Jude complained. He moved forward out of his seat, frowning at the teacher as he leaned across the aisle. "Can't we drive faster?"

"Mr. Charlie's job is to get us home safely. He can't do that if he drives too fast. Stay in your seat and try to relax," she said, gesturing for the boy to move out of the aisle.

"I love riding in buses. There's no seat belt," he said, jumping in the seat with his feet in the aisle.

Rachel sighed. So much for having the calm students. It would be a long ride home. "Sit back. You'll go flying if we have to stop or hit a pothole..." She jerked sideways in her seat as the bus lurched in its lane. "See what I mean? Potholes. Bumpy roads. Sit back."

A murmur came from the front of the bus. A chill raced down Rachel's spine as the adults started calling the driver's name.

"Mr. Charlie!" one parent shouted. "Wake up!"

Rachel looked out the front window. They were headed toward a large tree, with no sign of slowing down. At this speed, they'd hit the tree in a few seconds. "Sit back and brace yourself," she yelled, throwing an arm out toward Jude, who was still leaning into the aisle while he stared out the window.

She heard a sharp crack as pain ran the length of her arm. She let out a gasp. The last thing she saw, before the world went black, was the terror on her student's face.

Chapter Twelve

Scott

Scott leaned back in his chair and closed his eyes. It had been a long day, and his shift wasn't over yet. He was taking advantage of a brief lull and hiding out in his temporary director's office.

They'd had the usual chest pains, respiratory illnesses and broken bones today. Since he was a pediatric doctor working in an all-ages emergency room, he focused on the kids and pre-teens. But he also helped with the overflow—teenagers and young adults first, then adults with minor problems.

There hadn't been many pediatric emergencies today. Instead, he'd dealt with a twenty-year-old's alcohol poisoning and a teenager who thought helmets were for wimps. Two vomiting patients was enough for one day. Wasn't it great that concussions and overindulging had the same symptoms?

Not that pediatrics was any better. If he'd surveyed a room full of kids in a doctor's waiting room, odds were high at least one of them had a barf bag.

Still, today's patients were a reason their hospital needed a pediatric unit. Kids shouldn't sit next to a twenty-year-old alcoholic. It was exhausting to watch patients' poor decisions play out. Give him a kid with a broken leg, or even an elderly stroke victim, rather than tourists with no common sense.

He kept his eyes shut and let himself daydream about Rachel for a moment. They were meeting again tomorrow. Compared to what he faced at work, the woman was a burst of sunshine. She never failed to cheer him up.

Scott cracked his eyes as his office door opened, then shut them again when his nurse walked in.

"Good, you found a minute to rest. I won't jinx us by saying things slowed down." Adam chuckled. "I'm sure the next batch of patients will be here soon."

Scott kept his eyes closed and nodded. "Just trying to recharge my batteries."

"I won't stay long, but I had a question about the fundraiser. You've confirmed the hotel?"

"I have."

"And the caterer needs their down payment…"

"I know." Scott waved Adam's concerns away. If only he could push his exhaustion away so easily. "Sorry. I should have replied to your emails. I've worked twelve-hour shifts all week. Tomorrow's my day off. I'll catch up on the gala details then. I'm meeting with Rachel, too. Look for more updates after we meet."

Adam hummed his consent. "Take time for yourself, too. I'll leave you alone now. Get some rest while you can."

Scott nodded again, still not bothering to open his eyes. Sometimes his brain needed to reset. He spent the entire day taking in visual information—charts, vital signs, a patient's behavior. A good doctor could make a tentative diagnosis after a brief look at their patient and basic vitals.

Having your senses primed and ready for action was exhausting.

Rachel appealed to his senses, he thought, letting his mind drift back to her. She was beautiful. Smart, too. She also enjoyed kids.

Scott worked with women who were smart and liked kids, but he'd never had the urge to date them. They all spent too much time together. Besides, what could you talk about with another nurse or doctor? They couldn't discuss their patients in public.

And it was no fun dragging your work home each night, rehashing emergencies and patients over the dinner table.

Now that he was settled in Sunset Cove, it was time to connect with the locals. Start thinking long term and find a few spare moments to date. Even though the hospital should be his top priority, he was lonely.

Scott thought about William. Their CEO had found time to date, marry, and start a family. Maybe Scott's hyper-focus on work wasn't such a good thing.

He didn't know if Rachel was the right person for him, but it would be nice to take her out to dinner. Find out if they had anything else in common.

Scott snapped out of his daydream as the intercom crackled to life.

All available medical staff to the emergency room. All staff to the emergency room.

His eyes whipped open. Scott was halfway across the room when the door flew open. Adam burst through the doorway. "You've got a bus full of children on the way. Minor injuries, except for the driver. Possible heart attack."

Scott flipped into emergency mode. "Pull together all the pediatric-trained staff you can find. We need people trained in treating children." He scowled, knowing that Adam wouldn't find more than one or two nurses to help keep this crowd calm. "How many?"

"Fifty-two kids and chaperones. Five with documented injuries. The rest are unknown. They climbed off the bus without help, though."

Scott held back a curse. Fifty-two people in a twenty-bed emergency room. "Bring me the known injuries, and cycle the rest through triage as quickly as possible. I want eyes on these kids."

He spent the next three hours focusing on the fourth graders of Sunset Cove Elementary School. These were Rachel's students—kids she cared about. He'd checked the current list of patients, and had been relieved that she wasn't on the list.

Dr. Smith was dealing with the adult chaperones. He hadn't reported injuries yet, aside from the bus driver.

Scott had a few head bumps to monitor. None of the kids had concussion symptoms so far, but it was better to play it safe and keep them under observation.

Another boy had fallen out of his seat and sprained his wrist. That was a simple enough fix. Kids healed quickly.

Scott rubbed his temple in slow, calming circles. There had been lots to do in a short time, but he was grateful things hadn't been worse.

One more kid to assess, he told himself.

He walked into the last room and pasted a reassuring smile on his face. "Hello, how are you? I heard you had an adventure on your trip today."

Scott stopped short as a wave of shock and fear washed over him. A young girl was sitting on the hospital bed, playing with a phone. She appeared fine.

But that wasn't what caught his attention. He turned his focus to Rachel Lancaster, who was curled up in the guest chair, a shade paler than her normal color. She was favoring her left arm.

Lots of people tried to hide their injuries. It was his job to notice those injuries by observing his patient.

A thin sheen of sweat covered Rachel's forehead. She held her arm stiffly, away from her body, as she shifted in the chair.

What was Rachel doing in this girl's room? And more importantly, how badly was she hurt? He pushed down a moment of panic and the urge to call for help. Panicking wouldn't solve anything. Scott tried to ignore his fear and focus on the task at hand—performing triage on the woman who'd drifted into his daydreams just a few hours ago.

Scott glanced down at the child's chart. Emily Wilde, age eleven. Rachel didn't have children. Why was she in Emily Wilde's chair when she should be in her own hospital bed? "Rachel. It's good to see you. Everything okay?" he asked, trying to keep his voice calm.

Rachel pinched her lips together and nodded. "I didn't want to leave Emily alone. We sat together on the bus. How's the driver doing?"

"Let's focus on you first," he said, observing her movements. He glanced through Emily's vital stats, happy with what he saw. His young patient could wait a few more minutes. "Emily's fine. The bus driver's in excellent hands. Rachel, you don't look so great. Does anything hurt?"

She shook her head. "Focus on the kids. I can wait."

Scott set down his clipboard with a clatter and stared at her. "Absolutely not. Were you seen by triage? How long have you been here?"

"Well, the ambulance brought us a few hours ago. I told the nurse I could wait." Rachel closed her eyes and took a shuddering breath. "Emily's mom asked me to sit with her. Mom works an hour away. She's stuck in traffic. We couldn't reach Emily's dad."

Scott felt dueling emotions of anger and frustration. He understood the urge to take care of patients first, and worry about your own needs later. He'd never worked through a broken bone, though—and Scott's gut told him Rachel had at least a hairline fracture, if not worse. Sprains and dislocations didn't cause Rachel's symptoms.

He sighed and reached for his phone, then pressed the button connecting him to Adam. His nurse had been running around the ward all afternoon, shifting his focus from child to child as they dealt with injuries.

"I'm in room twelve, Dr. Hart. Where do you need me next?"

"I need a wheelchair in room nineteen. Find me an adult bed as soon as possible."

"They just discharged the last school chaperone. I'll let Dr. Smith know."

Scott thanked Adam and tucked his phone away. "I'll have my nurse keep Emily company until her mom gets here. They're getting a bed ready for you across the ward."

"I can wait," Rachel insisted. She leaned forward and moaned, tucking her arm closer to her body.

"It won't hurt you to wait, but there's no reason to be in pain longer than necessary," Scott said, unwinding the stethoscope from around his neck and moving toward Emily. "You can stay until Emily gets a clean bill of health. Then it's your turn to visit Dr. Smith. He's an excellent doctor with lots of experience."

Emily's eyes widened, looking back and forth between the two adults as they argued. "Ms. Lancaster, I don't want you to be in pain. Why are you holding your arm like that? You said you weren't hurt!"

"I'll be fine," she reassured her student, gritting her teeth as she shifted her arm again. "I'm right where I should be. Here, with you. Your mom will be here soon."

What a stubborn woman, Scott thought, his fear giving way to admiration as Rachel continued to fight for her student. He leaned forward and listened to Emily's clear lungs and strong heartbeat. He did a quick neurological exam, then checked each of her limbs for pain or weakness. Once Scott was done, Adam moved forward with the wheelchair.

"Sorry, Rachel. Doctor's orders. I've got to listen to Dr. Hart." He eased her into the chair, helping Rachel brace herself without bumping her left arm.

She nodded, letting herself be wheeled away once Adam promised to return and sit with Emily.

"Your mom will be here soon, kiddo. I'll see you at choir practice," Rachel promised.

Scott frowned as Adam wheeled her toward the imaging room. He'd messaged Dr. Smith to request a STAT order for X-rays.

As she disappeared down the hall, Scott couldn't help thinking that Rachel was right. She had been where she belonged. If he was lucky enough, she belonged with him.

For now though, he needed to focus on the kids still in his care. Scott gave Emily one last smile of encouragement and headed down the hall to check his concussion patients.

Chapter Thirteen

Rachel

Rachel gritted her teeth as she was wheeled back from the imaging room. She didn't need a doctor to realize her arm was broken. It hurt like crazy, especially when she tried to move it. The pain had caused her to black out on the bus. Not a good sign.

Still, she would be fine. Bones healed. As long as her students weren't hurt, she'd throw herself in front of them any day.

A few minutes later, a silver-haired doctor was standing beside her. He introduced himself as Dr. Smith; his name tag said his first name was James.

Dr. Smith had ordered pain medication and gathered supplies after seeing the X-ray. Gently holding her arm in place, he wrapped casting material around her forearm. "I hear you're the town hero today. The bus company reviewed footage from the accident. If you hadn't stopped that boy from flying forward, he might have gone through the windshield. You saved his life."

Dr. Smith's expression turned stern for a moment as he finished wrapping the cast. "Next time, watch out for yourself, too. Stay in your seat. Tell the kids to do the same." His voice turned gentle again, the lines on his weathered face softening. "But you did a good job. The boy wasn't hurt. I hope that arm heals quickly."

Rachel stared at her left arm, now encased in purple fiberglass from her hand to just above her elbow. The cast was growing uncomfortably warm. "Thanks. How fast are we talking? How soon can I get this cast off?"

"That's up to the orthopedist. I'd guess about four to six weeks."

"Six weeks," she squeaked. Her breath came out in little bursts as she began to panic. She was in charge of the fun run this weekend. There was also choir rehearsal, and thirty kids to keep in line during those rehearsals. The gala was only a few weeks away.

"That won't work," she sputtered. "I'm a music teacher. I need both hands. We're teaching recorder, and I'm working on the hospital's gala. This cast needs to come off sooner."

Dr. Smith raised an eyebrow. "The cast can come off in a few weeks. You'll use a sling for a bit longer. Fractures take time to heal. If you rush the process, you'll only cause more pain for yourself. The bone might not set properly. You'll find yourself back where you started—in a cast, but this time after surgery to reset the bone."

Rachel flinched. "That doesn't sound fun."

"It's not." Dr. Smith grabbed the chair alongside the bed and pulled it to her side. "I appreciate everything you're doing for this town. Dr. Hart told me about our fundraisers and how hard you've worked. I can't make a bone heal. I can get you an appointment with the orthopedist, though. He can decide how long you need the cast. But you've got to take it easy. Pushing yourself too hard will just slow things down."

Rachel swallowed the lump in her throat and nodded. There was so much to do before this weekend's run. She had to sort shirts for the runners. Stuff goody bags. Check on her friends, to make sure they had finished their own jobs. But she'd play by the doctor's rules if it meant she'd heal as fast as possible.

So instead of arguing, Rachel did her best to smile. "Thank you for help. I'd appreciate that orthopedics referral."

Dr. Smith nodded and typed a few things into his computer, then turned back to Rachel. "The scheduling team should call soon. If you don't hear from them by tomorrow, their number is in your paperwork."

Tomorrow. A lump formed in her throat. She was supposed to meet with Scott tomorrow. They were planning the last details for the gala. What would happen now?

Even if the cast came off, she would still need a sling. She wasn't sure if she could conduct a choir like this. How could she lead a group of children, and turn pages of music, with just one hand? Things were about to get very tricky.

Speaking of tricky... Her stomach fluttered as she thought about the way Scott had looked at her. When he'd found her in Emily's room, she'd seen anger, concern, and even fear flash across his face. Only for a moment, though. He'd quickly slammed a guard down in front of his emotions.

Some people might say he had a good poker face. Rachel suspected it was his doctor's face. He would be an excellent poker player.

He'd looked concerned, for sure. But was he worried about her, or the fundraiser? There was no way to tell. All Rachel could do was meet him tomorrow. Maybe he'd want to replace her. She could find someone from the middle school to lead the choir.

Rachel's heart sank as she thought about handing the choir over to a co-worker. These kids had worked so hard. She didn't want to walk away from her students. They'd have to take this one step at a time.

When a nurse came in with discharge papers, Rachel rummaged through her bag for her phone. She planned to walk the halls, making sure every kid had a parent—but she also needed to secure a ride for herself. They had all arrived by ambulance, which meant her car was still at school.

She wasn't in the mood to walk. Rachel had already texted her friends, letting them know she was okay after the accident. She checked her messages now and saw that she had three offers for a ride home. She let out a sigh of relief. One problem solved.

"Thanks for dealing with all of us so quickly," she told the nurse. "You've got a great hospital and staff."

The nurse looked surprised but pleased. "We do our best! Hope your arm is better soon."

"Thanks." Rachel flinched and adjusted the sling she'd been given to hold the weight of the cast. It sounded like the sling would be her BFF for a while. This would get old fast. Still, things could have been much worse.

Instead of complaining, she stood up to address the nurse. "Are all the students home? A few were waiting for their parents before my X-ray. I don't want anyone left alone. And how is the bus driver?"

The nurse twisted her lips in a frown. "I can't give information about other patients. A lot of the kids have gone home already, though."

"That's great. Thanks again," Rachel said. She attempted to give the nurse a warm smile.

Rachel would sneak down the hallway to make sure Emily wasn't alone. With any luck, the room would be empty. Her student could be home by now.

Elementary students and parents filled the halls of the emergency room. She recognized a few and gave a wave with her right hand. Her focus remained on the end of the hall, where Emily and her mom headed toward the door. "Emily! Mrs. Wilde! Wait for me."

The young girl and her mother turned. "Ms. Lancaster! Are you okay? I was worried about you!"

Rachel gestured toward her sling and purple cast. "Just a minor break. It sounds like no one was seriously hurt. I need to find Mr. Charlie, though."

Emily's mom reached out to squeeze Rachel's uninjured hand. "Thank you for watching my daughter. You kept our kids safe and made sure they weren't alone. Even with a broken arm." Her voice hitched as she choked back tears. "I couldn't be there for my daughter, but I'm grateful that you could be. Thank you."

Rachel's face flushed with embarrassment. She'd do almost anything for her students, but today felt like the ultimate test. This must be what parents felt like—putting a child's needs first, even if that meant neglecting your own needs. "I'm glad I could help. These kids feel like my own children. I'd do almost anything for them."

Emily's mom gave her hand one last squeeze. She pulled out a piece of paper and scribbled down her phone number. "Please call me if you need anything. I'd like to make a few meals for you. It's the least I can do."

"Please, that's not necessary." Rachel blushed again. "I already have my favorite pizza place on speed dial, so it's not like that will change. But I appreciate the thought."

Her heart gave a little squeeze as Emily walked away with her mother.

Was this what it felt like to be a parent? she wondered again. Dreading that call in the middle of the workday. Hearing that your child needed you, but unable to get to them.

It wasn't Mom's fault she worked an hour away from Sunset Cove. Sometimes it seemed like having children was like handing a piece of your heart to your child and watching them walk away. Praying that they kept your heart (and themselves) safe.

Rachel was still watching the closed door when a large, warm hand rested on her shoulder.

"Are you okay?" Scott asked quietly. "I heard about the broken arm. You seemed upset about the kids, too."

"Of course I'm upset! It's my job to keep these kids safe, and I failed. I should have known the bus driver was ill." Rachel frowned, thinking about the last few hours. She'd give anything to go back and stop that bus.

Scott rubbed the stubble on his chin as he considered her words. "From what I heard, you didn't fail. You saved a child from serious injury. But what about you? How are you doing?"

She took a breath and tried to steady herself. "I'm okay, I think. I'm not sure what to do about this arm, though. We've got the fun run, choir practice, and the gala…"

Rachel took another shuddering breath and tried to hold back her tears. She would not to cry in front of Scott. "There are people depending on me, including you. I don't know how to keep everything together with just one arm."

"Stop." Scott spoke firmly, putting a hand on her shoulder. He stared down at her with a stern expression. No more poker face. "You don't have to tackle this alone. You have great friends. I can help, too. Isn't that how small towns work? We take care of each other." His voice turned gentle as he glanced down at his watch. "On that note, my shift ends in ten minutes. Sit down and wait."

"Wait for what?"

"For me, of course. I'll drive you home. Make sure you're settled. And I don't know about you, but I'm starving." The doctor smiled and put a hand on his flat stomach. "I'll find food for both of us. One less thing for you to worry about."

Rachel sat in the chair, stunned. She hadn't expected Scott's offer. Still, she'd be relying on her friends a lot over the next few weeks. If she could take one task off their plates, she'd do it.

She pulled out her phone to update her friends, then mentally went through the list of things she needed to do.

Contact her friends... done.

Check on her students... done.

Check on Charlie...

Rahel gasped as she thought about the bus driver. She stood up and chased Scott down the hall. "Wait! Come back!" Once she was standing next to him, Rachel lowered her voice. "Can you tell me anything about Charlie Campbell now? The bus driver. What happened to him?" Her voice trembled as she realized that her friends weren't all accounted for. Charlie was like family. She sent up a quick prayer that he was okay, then kicked herself for not demanding answers sooner.

Scott reached out and touched under her chin, guiding her face upward until they locked eyes. "I can't normally disclose patient information, but Charlie asked us to update the school. I was going to call the principal and bus company before we left. He had a heart attack, but Dr. Smith thinks he'll be fine. We rushed him into surgery and placed two stents."

Rachel all but sagged with relief. Charlie would be okay.

Scott looked at her carefully, then guided her back to the chair. "You've had a long day. Just rest. I'll call the school, then take you home."

She sagged back into the chair. Now that the last of her adrenaline drained from her body, Rachel let her eyes drift shut.

Her eyes flew open as Rachel realized what she'd agreed to. How had tonight's plans changed so drastically? She'd planned a quiet night with some pizza and paperwork while she unwound from the field trip.

Now Dr. Hot Scott was coming to her apartment. For dinner.

Chapter Fourteen

Scott

Scott juggled Rachel's bookbag and his own bag as they walked to his Jeep.

Seeing her in that hospital room had shaken him to the core. He'd dealt with countless injuries. People who were hurt or in pain. But seeing Rachel hurt had nearly broken him. He'd fought the urge to yell for help, to prioritize her care over everyone else in that building—and he wasn't even the adult doctor. Scott's job was to take care of kids.

He'd need to reflect on what that meant. Rachel was becoming important to him. Did he care about her? As more than a friend?

He slowed his pace, being sure not to rush Rachel as they walked across the employee parking lot. When they got to his vehicle, Scott opened the passenger door and gestured for her to enter. "Ladies first. Mind if I help you?"

Rachel nodded.

Scott gave her time to settle herself, then reached in to buckle the seat belt around her. He hesitated for a moment, realizing for the second time that her hair smelled nice. A subtle, flowery scent. It reminded him of spring. He cleared his throat and pulled away, moving back into doctor mode. "I broke my elbow in elementary school. It's hard to work with one arm. There's no shame in asking for help."

Rachel blushed at his nearness, but said nothing. Taking her silence as a sign to continue, he placed their bags in the back seat. Scott turned the ignition, then twisted to look at her. "Where am I taking you?"

She stared at the floor of the Jeep, examining her sneakers as if they held an important message. "Back to my apartment, I guess. If that's okay."

"Of course it's okay. Unless you'd rather have a friend take you home. I shouldn't have pushed to do it myself." He paused, trying to gauge her mood. *You shouldn't just invite yourself back to a woman's home.* He wasn't even sure where she lived. "Does this make you uncomfortable? I can drop you off at the bakery or a friend's house. Just say the word."

"It's fine." Rachel raised her chin, looking him in the eyes. "I appreciate the help. My car is at school, though. Just take me there. I'll drive myself home."

Scott examined her more closely. Not only was her arm in a sling, but the bags under her eyes matched her purple cast. She was clearly exhausted. "You must be ready to pass out. You shouldn't be driving." He wouldn't allow her behind the wheel. She'd be back at the hospital when she fell asleep in the car. His voice softened as he watched her try to remain poised and alert. "Let me take care of you. Just for one night."

Rachel sighed as a single tear fell down her cheek. "You're right. I shouldn't be driving. I live over on Shell Avenue, the last apartment in the cul-de-sac. Do you know where that is?"

"A few of my nurse friends live there." He shifted the car into drive and pulled away, tucking aside his relief that she'd agreed to be driven home. He'd examine his feelings about her later. Tonight, Scott just needed to know she was safe.

He drove toward the one development in town, stopping at each red light along the way. Sunset Cove was filled with quaint single-family homes. One neighborhood was devoted to apartments and more affordable living. Adam lived here, too. He'd thrown Scott a welcome party months ago.

It was a cute neighborhood. Lots of kids playing, and bicycles parked in front of every modern apartment building. The contrast to the rest of the town's historic homes was striking.

"This is me." Rachel pointed to the last complex in the row. "Park in the third spot. That's mine."

Scott pulled into the spot and shifted into park, then reached over to help Rachel unclip her seatbelt. "Give me a minute. Let me help you out," he urged, rushing around to her door.

Rachel accepted his hand as she struggled to climb out of the Jeep, then waited while he grabbed their bags.

"Where's your key?"

"In the front pocket," she said, gesturing toward her bookbag.

He found her key ring in the pocket. One key and a car fob. *Simple enough*, he thought. "Letting us into the house now," he announced, turning the key and pushing the door open. Scott gestured for her to go first, but didn't step across the threshold.

Rachel turned and looked at him. Puzzlement shadowed her face. "Are you coming in?"

"Only if I'm invited. I can be a chauffeur. Your caterer. Or anything in between. You tell me what you want."

His heart gave a squeeze as he watched the vulnerable woman stand inside her apartment. Despite not having time for a relationship, he was falling for her.

He was still a gentleman, though. That meant Rachel needed to take the first step.

Scott nearly sighed with relief when she nodded and stepped back to let him into the apartment. "Come in. It's a little messy. That won't change until school is over and I have two working arms."

He chuckled as he walked into the apartment, hoping to hide his growing attraction. This was a helping mission. Not a date. She'd had a rough day, and he wouldn't make it harder by changing the terms of their friendship tonight.

Scott set her bag on the kitchen barstool, then held out the car fob in a gesture of peace. "I'm getting your car now. Is that okay? And I'll bring back food. What's your favorite restaurant?"

His heart went out to Rachel as her eyes widened. She clearly wasn't used to being taken care of. That would need to change. It was time for him to stop hiding behind the fact that they worked together. Maybe, once her arm was healed, he could admit that he wanted more than friendship from her.

The past few weeks with Rachel had been amazing. He looked forward to every phone call, every email, every text. It was nice to have someone outside the hospital to connect with, even if they were working on his fundraiser together. He loved hearing stories about her students and her day. It made the highs and lows of a doctor's life more bearable.

Still, the sudden urge to be more than friends struck him speechless. He glanced around the apartment for a talking point. His eyes settled on the refrigerator, where a few restaurant menus were stuck to the side. "You like Joey's? They've got great pizza."

Despite her exhaustion, Rachel's face lit up with a smile. "I love Joey's. I spend at least half of my paycheck there. They're going to name a pizza after me one day."

Scott grinned. A beautiful, hard-working woman who loved pizza? Why had it taken so long to realize he was interested in her? "Tell me what the Rachel pizza looks like."

She laughed as she settled on the couch, then winced. She hoisted her cast and sling onto the armrest. "Nothing fancy. Just a hot wing pizza with grilled onions. It's delicious, though."

Scott rushed forward to help her. He grabbed a pillow from the couch and propped it under her arm. "How about I order that pizza? I'll get your pain medicine from the pharmacy while they make our food."

Rachel's head sagged back into the couch cushion behind her. She nodded weakly. "Thanks, that would be great. I think the pain pills are wearing off. Sorry to be so annoying."

"You're never annoying." He grabbed a blanket off the side of the couch and tucked her in. Rachel's eyes fluttered, then drifted shut.

She's a keeper, he thought, watching her fall asleep. She'd risked her life today for her students. Scott would do the same for a patient, if it came down to that.

He shook his head. It wouldn't take much for him to fall in love at this point. That scared him. He'd never been so infatuated.

Sure, he'd dated a few women. But he'd never risked more than a superficial relationship. There wasn't enough time, and he'd moved too often as he rose from medical student, to resident, to attending physician, to division head. As he watched Rachel's chest slowly rise and fall, he considered the sacrifices he'd need to make this work.

His gut said they would be worth it. He'd need to find time to build something with Rachel.

Just not yet. He wouldn't take advantage of Rachel while she was injured. After checking to make sure she was settled, he grabbed her keys and headed out the door.

Time to run a few errands.

Chapter Fifteen

Rachel

RACHEL'S EYES FLUTTERED OPEN. She was sitting on the couch. Why wasn't she in bed? And why was her arm...

She threw her head back and groaned as she remembered everything that had happened that day. The bus accident, the broken arm, Scott driving her home. She sat forward with a jolt, then steadied herself as pain shot through her arm.

Scott. Where was he? He knew where she lived now, and they were alone in her house.

Rachel fought back a moment of panic. Scott was nothing like the creepy men in the city who followed women home. He wasn't the dad from school, trying to drag her into his car. He was one of the good guys. She let out another breath and looked around.

While Scott wasn't there, he'd left a note beside her.
Pain medication on the kitchen counter.
Pizza in the fridge.
Your car's parked outside.
Text me when you wake up, even if it's late. Let me know you're okay.

Rachel's eyes watered again as she re-read the note. She didn't deserve to have friends like Scott.

Were they friends? They worked together, but she felt more attracted to him every time they met. She wasn't sure what to do, though. If he didn't feel the same way, things could get awkward.

His note left her even more confused. Did this mean he cared about her? Or was he just being friendly? From a practical standpoint, it made sense that he'd helped her. She was no use to him if she couldn't finish the two fundraisers she'd started.

Rachel struggled to open the pharmacy bottle. Thank goodness he'd gotten easy-open lids. Then she pulled up her texting app.

> Just woke up. Took a pain pill. Thanks again.

Scott

> Eat something with that pill.

Rachel let out a snort. Once a doctor, always a doctor. She made her way to the fridge, holding it open with her leg while she pulled the pizza box out one-handed. It took a bit of maneuvering, but she managed to slide a slice of pizza onto the paper plates he'd left on the counter.

Her mouth watered. He must have asked for a "Rachel" pizza. It was just the way she liked it.

She wrangled the plate into the microwave and set the timer as her phone rang. Scott's name and number flashed on the screen.

"Just checking in. Everything okay?"

"I'm heating some pizza now."

"Great. Eat food with that medication. You'll upset your stomach if you don't."

"Yes, doctor," she teased. "Thanks again for getting my food and medicine. I'll need my friends the next few weeks. Glad I didn't have to ask them for help tonight."

Scott hesitated. The line was silent long enough that Rachel thought they might be disconnected. But when he finally rejoined the conversation, he spoke with a gravelly voice. "I'm your friend too, Rachel. I don't mind helping, and want to know you're taken care of. In fact…" He hesitated again. "I'd like to take you out for dinner tomorrow."

Rachel had put the phone on speaker as she wrestled with the microwave again. His words started her, and she nearly dropped her plate. "Dinner. Why?"

Scott laughed. "Don't sound so shocked. We were already meeting, and you've got to eat. I'm guessing it's harder than normal to put food together. So let's eat and talk. Get you fed. Make sure you don't need anything, and figure out how this gala will work with only three arms between us."

This time, Rachel joined in his laughter. She couldn't help it. Tonight's worries melted away. She had her friends, and she had Scott. Maybe things wouldn't be easy, but she could work with that.

Chapter Sixteen

Scott

Scott collapsed into his chair and put his head down on the desk. Today had been tough. Even worse than the day before.

Events like yesterday's bus crash were hard enough to deal with. This morning, he'd send one of his patients to a bigger hospital. The boy had been in clear respiratory distress, with a history of oxygen desaturation and a repaired heart defect. Scott suspected the boy needed cardiac intervention sometime soon, but he couldn't make that decision here.

It was tough to admit you couldn't help someone, but moving the boy had been the right choice. He'd have a better outcome at a bigger hospital.

Scott lifted his head and shoved his hands against the desk, making his chair fly back. They needed specialists who could deal with kids like this. No one should travel frequently for good medical care. If they had a pediatric cardiologist, the boy could have stayed in town. Recovered from whatever caused his desats. Push off his next visit to the city for a little longer.

Scott grabbed his expansion notes. A cardiologist was on the list of specialists they hoped to bring to the new pediatric center, but when would that happen? Scott frowned when he saw cardiology was in their third wave of hiring. Unless they shattered their fundraising goals, it would be at least two years until someone was here to help heart kids.

I will beg and plead for money if I have to, he thought. *We need this wing built and staffed. Today, not two years from now.* They'd never be able to offer cardiac surgery. Those cases belonged at CHOP or Boston, where staff handled dozens of surgeries every week. But this county needed a cardiologist who could monitor children and guide treatments. It was hard enough to be a kid with heart issues. It was even harder when you added travel time to the situation.

Scott understood why Rachel had agreed to help with the fundraiser. This wasn't a career move. Not anymore. These kids deserved his help.

His mood lightened as he thought about Rachel and her passion for children. She made him forget years of training on how to be clinical and detached. This woman turned his world upside down. He was in serious trouble.

But did falling in love have to mean trouble? Life should be more than hard work and long hours. Most of the doctors he knew were married with families. Maybe it was time for him to find balance, too.

If he was lucky, he'd already found the person to make that happen.

Rachel seemed like a good woman. She was honest and hardworking. He admired that. Shouldn't every relationship be built on respect and shared values? He needed someone he respected and cared about.

He glanced at the clock. Time to leave—his shift had ended twenty minutes ago. Scott pushed his chair back in and gathered his things. He was almost out the door when Adam walked into the office, his arms overflowing with a stack of folders.

This wasn't a good day to add work at the end of his shift. Scott held back a sigh. Adam rarely dumped work on him, so this must be important. "What's this?"

"It's the recruitment files you asked for. These are the top pediatric specialists in the area, sorted by their likelihood of commuting or moving to Sunset Cove."

Scott grabbed the bottom folder. These were trauma doctors and surgeons. He flipped through the pile of resumes and work histories. "Impressive. Let's go through these files next week. Then we'll contact our top choices and invite people for interviews. I've had a few doctors ask about the new wing, but it's time to play a more active role."

Adam nodded and leaned against the doorframe. "Schedule a time in your calendar. We can talk about which candidates to prioritize." The nurse crossed his arms and examined his friend's face more carefully. "How are you doing? Yesterday was rough. Doc Smith said Rachel broke her arm."

"We transferred a patient today, too. They couldn't get the care they needed at Sunset. Not yet, anyway."

Adam made a face. "I heard about it. He wasn't my patient, but it's never easy to send someone away. It's our job to get them the best care though, right? Even if that means we're not the ones providing the care."

Scott sighed. His nurse was right. There was no room for ego in an emergency room. If his hospital couldn't handle a patient, it was irresponsible to keep them.

It was even more irresponsible to accept their limitations. He was honor-bound to grow this hospital into a better place for medical care.

He rubbed a hand over his tired eyes, then slid the folder of resumes into his bag. "Thanks again. I'll go over this list tonight. After I meet with Rachel."

Scott expected Adam to nod and walk away. Instead, his co-worker stayed in the doorway, blocking him from leaving. "It's not my place to say this, but you're wearing yourself too thin. We need you for the long haul. Not a bright flash that gets this unit open before you burn out. Look through the files. Don't forget to relax tonight, though. Have a little fun with Rachel. Not every minute needs to be dedicated to your patients."

"I can't go drinking. I'm on call," he reminded the nurse. "Until we build up our staff, I'm always on call."

Adam tilted his head and continued to watch Scott's reaction. "Look at the doctors in the front folder. They're not specialists. They're generalists who could work in the ER. If we hired one more emergency room physician and a few pediatric nurses, we'd double our pediatric staff. It could help your sanity. And your patients."

Scott chuckled as he considered Adam's words. The man never failed to surprise him. Adam was right, too. Hiring just one pediatrician would take an immense burden off his shoulders. Scott was so focused on growing their specialities that he'd failed to remember how important emergency care was for the community. It was often their first stop, their first access to medical care.

He pulled out the folder and opened it again, taking his time with the first pages. Adam had printed pictures of most of the candidates, and Dr. Sonya Epstein smiled brightly from the first page. She was an emergency room physician and specialized in pediatrics. She'd trained at Boston and Hershey. Both excellent hospitals.

More importantly, Dr. Epstein had grown up in Sunset County, New Jersey, and earned her degrees at Rutgers. They could invite her to move back home.

Scott closed the folder and grinned. "You may be on to something. I'm not sure what I'd do without you."

Adam grunted and pushed away from the doorframe. "You'd manage. It's time to build our team, though, and stop putting so much pressure on you. We'll talk next week, then meet with the CEO and human resources."

Scott walked out of the hospital with a newfound spring in his step. They were on the right track. He'd review the files in his bag, then enjoy tonight's dinner with Rachel.

She still needed to make the first move. He could be patient. Rachel was juggling a lot, and Scott didn't want to push her too hard.

But for the first time, Scott hoped his career wouldn't be the only priority in his life. Scott smiled as he rolled down his Jeep's windows, letting the warm spring breeze rush inside.

Dinner with a beautiful woman put everything in perspective.

Chapter Seventeen

Rachel

RACHEL GLANCED AT THE notebook in front of her, resisting the urge to flip it open and start talking about work. Instead, she turned her gaze to the ocean and watched the waves crash against the shore. Anything to distract her from the handsome man across the table.

Scott had stuck to his promise of meeting over dinner. This was the first time they'd met outside the hospital or hotel ballroom. The Cove was the most popular fast-casual restaurant in Sunset Cove.

This was also their second time sharing a meal, but something felt different. Maybe it was the new location—or the way Scott had treated her last night. Rachel was struck by how sweet Scott had been. He'd tucked her in to sleep on the couch, making her as comfortable as possible, then found everything she needed for a restful night.

It had been a long time since someone had taken care of her.

Still, last night didn't mean anything. Rachel was attracted to Scott, and who wouldn't be? He was a handsome man. Kind and smart. That didn't mean their feelings were mutual.

They'd only gone to The Cove. It wasn't the fanciest restaurant in town. The Cove didn't even have indoor seating. It was all outdoors, just a few yards from the shoreline. Nothing romantic about it, Rachel assured herself.

That was fine. They didn't need to meet at a romantic restaurant. They were here to discuss work.

Rachel stayed lost in thought until Scott opened the folder in front of him and cleared his throat. She pivoted toward him, noticing that his light blue eyes sparkled like the ocean. Yes, he was attractive. But what could she do? They working together, and neither one of them had time to date.

Scott seemed more cheerful today, but remained focused on their task. "We've covered most of the gala details. You have thirty-two people in the choir, including yourself. I'll have snacks and drinks for the kids and parents while they wait. They're all welcome to join the crowd after they perform, but I don't think the kids would enjoy themselves." He smiled, his eyes crinkling with humor. "My CEO added champagne, scallops and lobster bites to the menu. So much for keeping it kid-friendly."

Rachel laughed, determined to enjoy this lighter side of Scott. None of her students would go to the gala. She'd already explained that they needed tickets to mingle. "Snacks and drinks would be great. Nothing staining, though. I don't need punch-covered kids on your stage."

"White grape juice and water," he agreed. "We'll save snacks for after the performance. Give them something to look forward to. In any case, we've handled most of the details. We just need to talk about you."

Rachel set her bottle of water down with a thump. This was it. Despite his promise to work things out, Scott was going to fire her. Could you even fire a volunteer? She wasn't exactly being paid.

So much for thinking he was attractive. He was about to dump her for another musician. One with two working arms.

Not that she blamed him. Anger and guilt mixed together, along with a curious amount of grief. She'd been looking forward to helping with the gala.

"Whoa, whoa." Scott held his hands up in defense, clearly reading the emotions as they flashed across her face. "It's going to be okay. I'm not sure why you're upset. I just want to help." He glanced at her purple cast and frowned, then rested a hand on her uninjured arm. "Do you need an assistant? Someone to turn the pages on your music stand? Or my tech guy could put everything on a screen. You can turn pages with one tap. Just tell me what you want."

Rachel commanded her eyes to stay dry. She kept the tears at bay, but couldn't keep her voice from wavering. "I thought you'd want to replace me. I can find another choir director to step in. The kids are almost ready, but they'll understand if someone else needs to lead them."

Scott frowned and squeezed her hand. "You deserve to finish this. Unless you want to step down, of course."

Rachel thought about the panic she'd felt after visiting the Golden Tides. Why had she been so afraid? She was proud of how hard her kids had worked. She was proud of herself, too. Rachel had never done something this big before, and these kids sounded fantastic. "No, I'm not stepping down." She raised her chin in defiance. "I thought you might replace me, though."

Scott rubbed a thumb over her hand, then gave it another squeeze. "You're not replaceable," he said softly. "Even with one arm, you're worth more to me than ten other music teachers. I hope you realize that."

A spark of electricity flew up Rachel's arm. "No one's called me irreplaceable before," she admitted, avoiding Scott's eyes. Her mind went blank with static as she considered what to say next.

A waiter broke the awkward silence. "Here we go! One Sunset Burger, chicken fingers, two orders of fries, and two chocolate milkshakes." He set the food on the table, then pulled out two straws. "Can I get you anything else?"

Scott glanced up at the waitress and smiled. "This is great, thanks." He pushed the chicken fingers and a bag of fries toward Rachel.

She mentally shook off her embarrassment, determined not to spoil the mood. They were working together for a few more weeks. There was no time for awkwardness. "No burgers for me right now," she joked, gesturing as Scott used both hands to pick up the enormous burger. Sauce dripped down his hand and onto the plastic wrapper. "I'll stick to finger food."

Scott's eyes lit up with humor. He took another bite of burger, then reached for the pile of napkins as he chewed and swallowed. "It's nothing a fork and knife can't solve. You might need some help cutting up food, though." He watched her take a bite of chicken, then set it down to fumble one-handed with her milkshake. "You'll need a plan, a way to adapt your to-do list. What still needs to be done for the school's fundraiser?"

Rachel groaned as she thought about the boxes of race shirts that arrived on her doorstep that morning. Her neighbor had dragged them into her apartment, but each shirt belonged in a bag with the runner's name and a goodie bag. "The broken arm complicates things. I'll call my friends. We can have a work party tomorrow."

"Why don't I bring people over to help? Let your friends focus on their own tasks for this weekend. You can get to know my co-workers, too." Scott smiled and gestured toward her with a fry. "They're impressed by the work you've done for the children's ward. Adam is one of your biggest fans."

Rachel raised her eyebrows. "I've got fans?"

"Of course. The more money we can raise for the hospital, the faster we can build our network and help the kids in this community." Scott nodded as he took another slurp of milkshake. "Besides, you got hurt protecting your students. That earns respect in the pediatric world. We're happy to help. And it would be nice to spend time with you, besides planning the gala."

Rachel's heart beat faster. He enjoyed spending time with her? Her face flushed as she nodded. "Sounds like a plan. I'll order hoagies for everyone. What time does your shift end tomorrow?"

· ♥ · ♥ · ♥ · ♥ · ♥ ·

Laughter filled Rachel's small apartment, wrapping around her like a warm blanket. She hadn't had so much fun since... well, she wasn't sure.

The two men folding shirts jockeyed for position, arguing over whose turn was next. Rachel couldn't help but laugh. "We've got dozens of shirts left. There's lots of work to go around," she teased, chuckling at Scott's and Adam's antics.

It seemed both men had a strong competitive streak. Scott said they worked well together, but outside the hospital? She shook her head and tried not to giggle. They were both determined to impress Rachel tonight. As a result, they were moving a lot slower than she'd expected—but also having a lot of fun.

Fun was important. Rachel hadn't realized how lonely she was in her apartment. Her new friends could stay as long as they wanted.

It was a shock to realize how much she enjoyed spending time with Scott. She'd seen his professional side and spent hours working on the gala with him, but he was fun and friendly outside work. It was hilarious watching him argue with Adam over who could fold shirts faster.

"Rachel, you be the judge. I'm faster." Scott whipped a shirt in the air and slid it into the labeled bag.

Adam sighed and picked up another shirt. "Stuffing them in the bag doesn't count. You need to tuck and fold. It's like making a hospital bed—neatness matters. I do hospital beds all day. Doctor Hart doesn't dirty his hands with bed linens."

The two men elbowed each other, making her shake her head again. She stepped away from the group to check her phone. Two texts from Brook, asking how she was doing. She dictated a reply:

> I've got Scott and his friend folding shirts.

Brook

> Hot Scott folding laundry. Very domestic.

Rachel chuckled and closed her text messages, then checked the time on her phone. Her eyes widened. It was almost nine o'clock. They still had lots of shirts to fold and goody bags to stuff, and they all worked tomorrow morning. "All right, boys. Let's bring it together. Scott, you've got Quinn Anderson. Youth medium. Marie Anderson needs a youth large."

Each man reached for the right-sized shirt and folded it. Rachel braced her cast against the sheet of name labels and pulled Quinn and Marie's labels off the sheet, then stuck a girl's name on each bag. She smiled as she pictured Harry's granddaughters. Rachel was glad they'd be in the fun run. She knew Harry would wait at the finish line, cheering them on.

Rachel kept them working for the next twenty minutes, calling out sizes and sticking labels on bags while the men folded and stuffed each shirt into a bag. Next, they sat down to fill goody bags with pencils, a water bottle, and cereal bars—all donated by local businesses.

When they were done, nearly two hundred bags sat in boxes by her door. Scott would take them down to her car before he left. Rachel would sacrifice some trunk space until race day, but it was the most logical solution. It wasn't like she could carry them around with one arm.

They lounged on the couch, content to be quiet for the first time that night.

Adam spoke first, from the far side of the couch. "That was fun. I'm glad to officially meet you, Rachel. Thanks again for helping us raise money."

"I'm happy to help. Have you worked at the hospital long?"

Adam shook his head. "Scott advertised for a pediatric nurse. I've always loved the beach. Thought it would be fun living near the shore. I'm super excited about the new pediatric ward. I've never built anything from the ground up, you know? This feels important."

He glanced down the length of the couch to Scott and Rachel. They weren't quite touching, but they were a lot closer than Adam was to them. "It's time for me to leave." He gave them both a cheeky grin. "Thanks again for the food. I'm headed out. Don't stop the party for me, though."

Rachel blushed as she realized how close she was sitting to Scott. It hadn't been intentional. She bolted upright and moved between the two men, not wanting to give Scott the wrong impression. Rachel wouldn't throw herself at him. That would just be embarrassing.

Even if he was the nicest guy she'd met in a while. And one of the most handsome...

Rachel cleared her throat. "Thanks again for your help. Can I make either of you something before you leave? I have coffee and iced tea."

Adam shook his head and smiled. "I'll stop by Saturday to help with the run. Let me take a box to your car while I'm leaving." He hefted the box into one hand, then turned the doorknob to her apartment. "See you in the morning, Scott."

Scott nodded. "Thanks again." He gave his friend a hearty pat on the back. "See you at seven. Let's hope it's a quiet day."

"It's never a quiet day." Adam rolled his eyes as he walked out of the apartment. He closed the door, leaving Rachel and Scott alone.

Chapter Eighteen

Scott

With Adam gone, the space seemed quieter. Smaller, too. Like the universe was using all its gravity to pull Scott toward Rachel.

That's not how physics works, he grumbled to himself. *Pull yourself together.*

Scott grabbed the second box of shirts and followed Adam out the door. "Be right back," he called over his shoulder.

His friend was loading the first box into Rachel's trunk. Adam seemed surprised to find Scott outside with him. "I left you alone with a pretty girl. Put that box down and go inside."

Scott set his own box in the trunk and frowned. "Is that why you left?"

"Yes. You don't need a third wheel." Adam rolled his eyes. "She obviously likes you. Take her out for a movie. Or find a rom-com to stream."

"It's too late for the movies." Scott checked the time, considering his options. "We could go for ice cream, though. Would she like that?"

Scott wasn't sure what to do with Rachel. They always worked when they got together. Even tonight, they'd met to finish a task. It felt good to work toward a common goal. But how did you simply spend time with someone?

Scott resisted the urge to pound his head against the car. He'd been single for too long. Things shouldn't be this complicated.

Adam laughed at his pained expression. "When was the last time you asked a girl out?"

"This wouldn't be a date. We're friends."

"But you like her." Adam didn't bother asking. He stated his observation as if it was common knowledge.

"Of course I like her. Rachel's smart. She cares about kids."

"She's beautiful, too. Get your butt back inside." Adam slapped Scott on the shoulders and spun him around to face the apartment. "Invite her out for a treat. The ice cream parlor would work. Not too quiet, but it's a good space to talk to someone."

Scott nodded and headed back into the apartment, rolling his eyes. Who needed a matchmaker like Nick Butler when he had Adam on his side? The town was filled with people giving advice on his dating life.

When he got back inside the apartment, Rachel was fussing with sheet music. The woman never rested. She reminded Scott a lot of himself—he liked to stay busy. The thought made him smile.

He walked over to Rachel and sat down on the kitchen bar stool. "I had fun tonight. Are you caught up with your work?"

She nodded, frowning at the papers in her hand. "I think so. We're ready for this weekend. I've got decisions to make for the children's choir, but I don't need help with that. Unless you want to go over song titles now. But it's getting late." She glanced at the clock, her face covered with guilt. "I've kept you out too long. We've both got an early start tomorrow."

They could stay in the apartment and talk about the choir. That felt like a wasted opportunity, though. If he wanted to get closer to Rachel, they needed to talk about each other—not just the fundraiser.

Still, Scott knew what it was like to be overworked and overwhelmed. He didn't want to stop Rachel from getting work done tonight.

An idea came to Scott. He snapped his fingers. "Pack up this sheet music," he announced. "Bring it along. We're going out for ice cream. We both deserve a treat tonight."

A smile stretched over Rachel's face. "I haven't had ice cream in ages."

"I've heard good things about Sunset Cove's ice cream parlor. Have you been there?"

"Scoops and Cones is the best. You haven't lived until you've tried their peanut butter fudge rocky road." Rachel slid her music into a folder and tucked it inside her bag, continuing to grin.

Scott's mouth watered. Who was this woman, and why was she perfect? Hot wing pizza and rocky road ice cream. Clearly, he needed to keep her around. "Let's go. I'm ready to start my life at Scoops and Cones."

Scott walked back to their table with an enormous bowl of ice cream. The sweet treat was dotted with chocolate chunks and swirled with peanut butter and fudge.

Rachel raised her eyebrows. There was one bowl and two spoons. "I thought doctors would want separate bowls."

He shrugged and handed her a spoon. "What's a few germs between friends? Besides, we spent the last few hours together. If you've got any respiratory viruses, you've already shared them with me."

Scott held back a laugh as Rachel stared at him in disbelief. He dropped his poker face and grinned. "I'm joking," he assured her. "I didn't know what size bowl you wanted, and knew I'd get too much ice cream for myself. One large bowl seemed like a good compromise."

It also makes tonight feel more like a date, he reflected. Scott hadn't planned it that way, and he felt guilty now for getting one bowl to share. Tonight was about getting to know Rachel—not pushing her too fast. Best to build a solid friendship first.

The thought of taking things slow made Scott squirm. He'd never felt attracted to someone like Rachel. The woman made him want to jump in feet first, not worrying about where he might fall. It was a surprising change for a doctor who approached every situation with caution.

Rachel took the first bite of ice cream and moaned. "It's better than I remember. Thanks for bringing me here tonight."

"You deserve a break. The past few days haven't been easy."

Rachel held up a spoon and pointed it at Scott. "Yesterday, you treated four dozen students after a bus accident. Then you walked to the school and drove my car home. You also worked a twelve-hour shift today, then spent hours labeling shirts and stuffing bags for my school's fundraiser. You need a break, too."

He shrugged. "It's part of the job. You get used to it." Scott thought he'd adapted to the emotional trauma and rush of the emergency room—until he saw Rachel in the hospital bay. He distracted himself with a bite of ice cream, hoping to shove aside the image of Rachel cradling her arm.

It worked, at least a little. His eyes popped open as the flavors hit his tongue. "This stuff is fantastic. Why aren't you here every night?" He patted his stomach and chuckled. "They might have to roll me out."

"It would be worth it," she conceded, taking a second scoop of ice cream. "What are we talking about tonight? The gala songs, right?"

"Sure, let's get that done. You deserve a night off, though. We're giving ourselves five minutes to talk about the fundraiser, then moving on."

Rachel furrowed her brow, then shrugged. "We're not taking a break if we work the whole time. Fair enough."

"Four and a half minutes," he announced.

She laughed, opening her music folder. "I'm thinking of adding 'I Lived' by One Republic. I've got a strong soloist. It's a crowd pleaser. It's a song about hope, too—face your struggles head-on, and never stop living."

"I love that song." Scott's eyes brightened, reaching out to squeeze her hand. "And you're right. It's perfect for a children's hospital. Three minutes left. What else do you have?"

Rachel grinned and flipped to the next page. "'This is Me' from 'The Greatest Showman.' A few short solos, and I love the message. It gives me shivers when the kids sing it, too."

Scott glanced down at the music and nodded. "You've done a great job bringing this all together." He met her eyes and smiled gently. "I'm glad you stumbled into my emergency room after the Easter egg hunt. It's like we were destined to meet."

Rachel blushed. Scott wanted to kick himself for the way he worded his compliment. He only meant to say that they worked well together. They'd even impressed the hospital's CEO.

Scott wouldn't take back his words, though. They *were* destined to meet, and not just to raise money for the hospital. He needed to tell Rachel how he felt. Eventually.

But before things turned too serious, it was time to change the subject. "That's the end of our work time," he teased. "Now we take a break. Tell me about yourself. How did you end up in Sunset Cove?"

If Rachel was surprised by the change in conversation, she didn't show it. "I grew up in Michigan, but spent summers here with my great-aunt. Crime is out of control in my hometown. I needed a change of pace."

"Did your great-aunt leave you a house?" he asked, trying to connect the dots. "You live in an apartment now."

"She passed away a decade ago." Rachel waved her spoon around as she talked, a habit she'd learned since moving to New Jersey. "She left me some money. I used it to make a deposit on my apartment. It wasn't enough money to buy a house, but it was enough to get settled. I passed the New Jersey licensing test before I moved. By the time I got here, I had a teaching job lined up."

Scott nodded, impressed. "You're a real go-getter. Someone who sinks their teeth into a goal and doesn't let go until it's met."

"I wouldn't go that far. My goal for this week was to wrap up practice and teach my students the last song for the concert." She held up her cast. "No more recorders for me. Sometimes you've got to pivot."

He was glad to see Rachel taking her injury in stride. Broken bones needed time to heal. Making yourself miserable didn't change anything. He tipped his head toward her. "Here's to rocking your new goals."

Rachel blushed again, staring down at the ice cream. "What about you? How did you end up in Sunset Cove, in charge of a new children's division?"

"Like I said, it was a good career move at the time."

"'At the time.' Are you questioning that move?"

Scott scooped up another bite of ice cream, taking time to think over his response. "No regrets. I just thought this would be a stepping stone. Build the children's division, grow it for a few years. Leave my mark on the project. Use it as a catapult to a bigger hospital." He looked around at the small ice cream parlor and shook his head. "I'm not sure what I want now. Sunset Cove is growing on me. I might stay for a while."

He thought about his CEO's story. William had moved to Sunset Cove, met a woman, and never left. Scott hid a grin as he took two more bites of ice cream. For the first time, Scott wondered if he'd have the same fate. Falling in love wasn't the worst thing that could happen.

Rachel held up her spoon in a mock toast. "Here's to landing in Sunset Cove, and sticking around."

Here, here, he thought, gently tapping the handle of his spoon to hers. "To sticking around, and to all our adventures to come."

Chapter Nineteen

Rachel

"Great job, boys and girls! Let's try that song one more time."

Rachel grinned as her students took sips of water and prepared themselves for another round. These kids weren't afraid of hard work. They rehearsed each song multiple times during practice, trying to perfect the smallest details. It was clear they were practicing at home, too. Rachel was so proud of her students.

She lifted her good arm to flip the music back to the beginning, then nodded to Isaac, who turned on her music player.

Rachel pointed to each group of students as it was their turn. This was a tricky song. Each group sang at a different time, which meant that everyone needed to focus. She gestured toward the boys' section, then flailed her arm back to the sheet music to turn the page.

Pages fluttered to the floor as she hit them with her cast and sling. Rachel held back a groan, but tried to stay in the moment. She could conduct a song from memory. This was the whole point of rehearsals—being prepared to perform, no matter what happen.

Dropping your music, and losing the ability to use one arm, was kind of worst-case scenario.

Stop it, she told herself. *So many things could have gone wrong.* One of her students could have been hurt or killed. Jude had almost flown through the windshield. He could still be in the hospital, trying to overcome catastrophic injuries. Or worse.

Rachel choked back tears as scenarios swirled through her mind. No, a broken arm wasn't the worst thing that could happen. She needed to pull herself together and finish this song.

When the song ended, Rachel tried to smile at her students. But they knew something was wrong. Thirty faces stared back at her with looks of concern.

Emily Wilde edged out of her chair and approached the teacher cautiously. "Are you okay? Did you hurt your arm again?"

Rachel's heart ached from the young girl's concern. It was Rachel's job to take care of these students—academically, physically, and emotionally. Now they were stepping up to take care of her.

At least her students were kind, caring individuals. One goal met.

Rachel wiped the tears from her eyes. "Sorry about that. I'm a little tired and emotional today. We all have days like that, right?" Her students nodded, some more hesitant than others. "I could use some help, though. Can someone turn the pages? I can't move my wrist, and I can't bend my elbow. I'll figure out a solution, but could someone help me today?"

Her eyes watered again as every student's hand shot into the air.

Jude stood up and lumbered forward, his most recent growth spurt making him look like a puppy growing into its paws. "It's my fault you're hurt," he mumbled. "I want to turn the pages."

"Not your fault. We both should have been sitting in our seats. I'm just glad you weren't hurt." Rachel smiled at him, hoping to relieve some of the boy's guilt. She grabbed a pencil and made marks on each page. "Turn the pages when we hit these marks. I'll give you a nod when it's time. Sound good?"

Jude's head bobbed in agreement.

The choir went through the song a final time. There was no sense in getting frustrated with her situation. It wouldn't change anything. She needed to adapt and move on. As Rachel nodded her head at Jude, he smiled and turned the page. He never stopped singing, his rich voice mixing with the students in front of him.

Rachel was pleased with the songs she'd chosen. Scott seemed to like them, too. Each piece was cheerful and upbeat, just like she imagined the children's ward.

She thought back to her tour of the construction site. The finished ward would be comfortable, colorful and playful. It should fill a child with hope and a bit of cheer, making a scary trip a little easier. That was the mood she'd hoped to strike with her songs.

Rachel raised her hand to clap for the students, then held back a groan. No more clapping for a while. Instead, she raised her voice over the students' excited chatter. "Excellent job! You've all worked so hard. Keep practicing at home. I've also got our schedule for the summer. We'll meet a few times after school ends. You're really going to impress the hospital's donors."

The students grabbed their bags and headed out the door, each accepting a printed schedule from Rachel as they left the classroom.

Emily stayed behind. After everyone else had left, Rachel sat in a chair and patted the seat next to her. "Now it's my turn to ask what's wrong. Are you okay?"

Emily stared at the floor and nodded, but nothing about her posture said she was fine.

"Are you sure? You don't have to talk about it. I'm here for you, though. I hope you know that."

Emily took a shaky breath and nodded again, frowning. "One of the fifth graders made fun of us today. He said singing's for babies. When I told him choir is awesome, he took my lunch money."

Rachel let out a huff and walked over to her desk. She pulled out the granola bar she kept for emergencies and held it out to Emily.

"That's not okay. We're going to tell Principal Sawyer. It won't happen again. But take this—you should eat something."

Emily blinked back tears and unwrapped the granola bar. "I don't think singing is for babies. I think the choir is great. It's not fair that people make fun of us."

"It's never okay for someone to make fun of you. If they're your friend, they should be okay with your hobbies. If they're not your friend, they should mind their own business." Rachel sat back down and sighed. "I'm glad you stood up for yourself, though. That's hard."

Emily took a bite of the granola bar and frowned. "You're being bullied too, aren't you? People aren't nice."

"People can be mean sometimes, but I'm not being bullied." Rachel frowned and put her hand on Emily's arm, praying that the student wasn't talking about her own dad. "I have friends, and I like the people I work with. No bullies."

"But you are!" Emily stood up, letting granola crumbs drop to the floor as her face hardened in anger. "I'm sorry for how my dad acted. He got mad when you wouldn't go out with him. He makes fun of the choir now, too. And he laughed at me when I told him to stop. He's picking me up today, since it's his turn. You should stay inside."

Rachel's heart felt like it might crack into two pieces. No child should need to stand up to their parents. Moms and dads should support their kids, not tear them down.

They definitely shouldn't make a child feel uncomfortable in school.

She did her best to hide her emotions, nodding slowly. Emily's dad was downright creepy. It wasn't her student's job to protect her, though. As much as Rachel wanted to hide from Mr. Wilde, getting students home was part of her job.

Rachel pasted on a bright smile and shook her head. "It's not your fault, Emily. And it's fine. The principal's helping with pickup today. My friend Brook will be there, too." She glanced at the clock, then stood up and gestured toward the door. "We should go. My friend and Mr. Sawyer are waiting, and your classmates want to go home. They can't leave until we're all ready."

Emily didn't look convinced, but she grabbed her bag and moved toward the door.

Determined to cheer up her student, Rachel kept up a conversation as they walked down the empty halls. "What did you think about practice today?"

"It was pretty good. I like the songs. And I'm really glad you can still be our teacher, even with a broken arm."

"A broken arm couldn't keep me out of this school." Rachel nudged Emily with her purple cast and smiled. "I'd miss you all too much."

They walked in silence, down the long hallway and toward the front doors. When they were nearly there, Emily stopped. She held up her arm, gesturing for Rachel to stop with her.

"Thanks again. I was really scared after the bus accident. I'm glad you stayed with me, even though you hurt your arm. Dad says I should have sat by myself while you got your arm fixed. But I'm glad you stayed. And I hope your arm gets better soon."

Rachel's temper rose as she thought about Emily's father. He hadn't come to the hospital. Rachel didn't mind sitting with a student—even with a broken arm—but Mr. Wilde hadn't returned the hospital's phone call.

"Mom and Dad got into an argument about you," Emily said, lowering her voice. "I'm not supposed to say anything. They argue about everything, though."

Rachel's stomach sank as she processed Emily's words. Divorces were never easy, but they were worse when a child was involved. She lowered herself to one knee and looked Emily in the eyes. "As long as you are my student, you will never be alone. I'm glad I waited with you. It's scary to be alone. And can I tell you something? I was scared, too. I was glad you kept me company."

A single tear ran down Emily's cheek as she jumped toward Rachel, wrapping her arms around her teacher. "Thank you," she mumbled against the older woman's hair. "I'm glad you're my teacher."

Rachel fought back her own tears as she angled her sling away from Emily and patted her on the back. Hugs from students were the best. She didn't get many hugs from the bigger kids, which made them even more special.

Emily was a special kid.

Rachel steadied herself, then stood up and gestured toward the front doors around the corner. "And I'm glad you're my student. Why don't we go outside, and I'll see you in music class tomorrow?"

Emily nodded and grinned, walking with a skip in her step as they met the other choir members and headed out the front doors. Principal Sawyer and Brook flanked them, both deep in conversation with the students.

But something was wrong. Emily's smile slid off her face and she skidded to a stop. Her dad had planted himself outside the doors, his arms folded.

"Pickup was ten minutes ago!" Cory yelled, grabbing Emily's bookbag to yank her forward. "I've got a date tonight, and now I'm gonna be late. Stupid choir practice."

Rachel flinched as Emily flew toward her dad, bumping into his leg. He grunted and pushed her away, then grabbed the bookbag again and pulled her to the car. "Come on. I don't have all day."

That was enough. Rachel stepped forward. She sensed her principal and friend stepping out of line behind her. "Mr. Wilde! How wonderful to see you," she said, fighting to keep anger out of her voice. "I'm sorry that practice ran over. We'll watch the time more closely next time. I'm not moving as quickly as I normally do."

His eyes roamed over her cast and sling, then up to Rachel's chest.

Yuck, she thought. *My eyes are up here.* Rachel put her good hand on her hip and watched as he let go of Emily's bookbag. The girl stared at the sidewalk, her cheeks bright red with embarrassment. If he treated Emily like this in public, how did he act at home?

Cory sneered at Rachel and gestured toward her cast. "Sorry about your arm. Sounds like my kid stopped you from getting it fixed. If I can help you…"

Rachel swallowed back the bile rising in her throat. Lots of friends and co-workers had offered to help her. Scott had taken care of her after she left the hospital. But none of them made her feel dirty, like this man's offer. "Thank you, but I'm fine."

"Are you sure?" Cory raised his eyebrows. His eyes darkened. He took a step toward her, lowering his voice. "I'm very helpful. We could drop Emily at her mom's house. I'll cancel tonight's date for you."

"While that's a very generous offer…"

"It's generous, but it won't be necessary," Brook announced, stepping between the two of them. "I'm taking care of Rachel tonight. Have a good day." She held out her hand, gesturing for him to get into the car.

Rachel sighed, torn between relief and disgust. How did Emily put up with this? What had she seen at her dad's house? She shuddered and sent up a prayer that the girl's home life would become safer, and soon.

Emily looked miserable as she climbed into the car, then waved out the window. "Bye, Ms. Lancaster. Thanks, Mr. Sawyer. See you tomorrow."

The rest of the students drifted toward their parents' cars, many with wide eyes. Rachel wondered how much the children had understood, or if they were just surprised to hear adults arguing. She hoped it was the second option. These kids were far too young to understand innuendos.

Once all the children were gone, the adults went back inside the building. Allen gave Rachel a grim smile. "That's one problem sorted."

"What do you mean?" Rachel could name at least two additional problems from this afternoon's events. She was worried about her own safety—and Emily's home life.

But Allen just twisted his face into a half-hearted grin. "By this time tomorrow, I'll have a dozen complaints against Mr. Wilde. Emily's mom asked the courts for full custody after the last incident, but she didn't have any evidence of wrongdoing. All those parents saw Emily being dragged toward the car, plus we've got it on camera. It's hard to stand back when we suspect students are being treated poorly. Now we have proof. I doubt Mr. Wilde will visit our school again."

Rachel let out a sigh as Brook wrapped her in a hug. Could it be that simple? Would this be the last time she faced Cory Wilde? She prayed the principal was right.

"We'll take care of Emily," Brook promised. "And we'll keep you safe, too. Let's go home."

Chapter Twenty

Scott

Scott looked around the gym at Sunset Cove Elementary School, his eyes widening as he took in the number of baskets Rachel's team had gathered for the raffle.

They'd filled more than a dozen tables with colorful baskets, each filled with prizes from the local community—baking lessons at Seaside Cupcakes, a gift certificate to the local lobster house, and baskets filled with art supplies and children's books.

Scott's heart swelled with gratitude. The town had worked together to make this raffle happen. His hospital couldn't grow without the community's support.

He grinned at a basket filled with a plush dolphin and a bottle of wine. There was also a voucher for a dolphin-watching ride, including breakfast for two and an hour-long trip around the cove.

Scott pulled out his tickets and stuffed a few into the jar for Joey's Pizza, then considered his options. If he won the boat ride, who would he take? He wondered if Rachel liked dolphins. He'd been looking for more excuses to spend time with her. This could be a way to thank her—for helping with the gala, but also for organizing the school's fundraiser. She'd done so much, even with a broken arm.

"If I were you, I'd put all my tickets in that one." Nick Butler appeared next to Scott, his hands stuck in his pockets and a wide grin across his face. "A sunrise boat ride, with breakfast and dolphins? Super romantic. You can take Rachel if you win."

"Still playing matchmaker." Scott shook Nick's hand, then looked at his raffle sheet. He had twenty tickets left. Could he win the boat ride with twenty tickets? "It would be a nice way to thank Rachel for her hard work. Do you think she likes dolphins?"

Nick shook his head. "It's not about the dolphins. It's a quiet, romantic outing. No talking about the hospital, or fundraisers. Just the two of you alone, getting to know each other. Seeing if sparks fly."

Scott chuckled and began tucking tickets into the raffle jar. "What if we're just friends?" he teased. "Two friends can watch dolphins. Even at sunrise." He stuffed his last ticket in the jar, then crossed his fingers behind his back for good luck.

"You don't use that many tickets for a friend," Nick noted.

"The raffle raises money for the hospital. I work there, remember? It's job security." Scott replied, resisting the urge to pull out his wallet. He could buy more tickets later, when Nick wasn't watching. No need to give his new friend more reasons to tease him.

His attempt at casualness didn't work. Nick threw his head back and laughed, then became serious as he focused on Scott again. "It's okay to like someone, especially someone as nice as Rachel. She cares a lot about her students. They're like her own children." He drummed his fingers on the table, then lowered his voice as a group of parents walked past them. "You wouldn't be here, trying to build a pediatric hospital, if you didn't care about kids. I still say you should go for it."

"Thanks, I'll keep that in mind. Rachel's my friend, though. I don't want to scare her away. Besides, we're both a little busy right now." Scott checked his watch and grimaced. He wouldn't be buying any more raffle tickets. "I'm meeting her outside in five minutes to set up the running course."

"It's your choice." Nick rubbed the back of his neck and frowned. "Look, I don't like to push. I tell guys to take it slow. But in this case, you need to speed things up. Rachel doesn't scare off easily, but she's so focused on her students that she doesn't notice the little things. You'll have to go big to get her attention."

Nick turned as a young girl ran up to him. "This is my daughter, Bree. Say 'hello' to Dr. Hart. I'm building his new hospital wing, remember?"

Bree nodded and grinned. "Hello, Dr. Hart. It's nice to meet you." The girl barely paused for breath before turning back to Nick. "Dad, can we buy tickets for the baking lessons? Ms. Brook is the best baker in town, and she says I can invite five friends if I win!"

Nick opened his wallet and pulled out a twenty-dollar bill. "Of course. Make sure you share these tickets with your sister. Do you need help?"

She grinned and took the money. "Thanks, Dad. I've got this."

Nick laughed as his daughter ran away, the bill flapping in her hand. "I'll need to supervise this from a distance. Raising kids is hard work, but it's the best work I've ever done. Just think about what I said."

He ambled across the length of the gym, stopping to stand next to his wife at the baked goods table. All of Rachel's friends were helping today, because that's what this town did. People worked together to get things done. This fundraiser wouldn't earn millions of dollars. But they'd still make a sizeable donation, based on the number of people streaming through the door.

He estimated that Nick's older daughter was eight or nine. Her sister was about two years younger. Old enough to be independent, but not old enough to be alone, even in a town like Sunset

Cove. Scott liked the way Nick handled the situation. He stood talking to his wife, monitoring his daughters while they enjoyed some independence.

He felt a stab of jealousy as Nick's daughters turned to wave at their parents.

Where had that come from? He'd never been jealous of someone before—especially parents. Even though he wanted children, he'd drive himself mad if he envied every family that walked through his hospital.

Scott pondered his reaction as Nick waved back and leaned in to give his wife a kiss. All this talk about matchmaking and small-town families was catching up with him. He furrowed his eyebrows as the girls ran back to their parents. It made a sweet picture.

He imagined Rachel carrying a little girl through the gym. The girl had his dark hair and her bright eyes.

The longing hit him like a brick wall. What if Nick was right? What if he needed to make his intentions known, and soon? Maybe letting Rachel make the first move was a mistake.

Scott wasn't used to hesitating. In the emergency room, he assessed a situation and took action. That skill saved children's lives.

He took a deep breath and steadied his nerves. He needed to tell Rachel how he felt. Ask her out on a date. Put it all out there and pray she said "yes."

Scott turned toward the door, prepared to find Rachel before they set up for the race. But there was a wave of people coming toward the raffle tables now, slowing his progress. He sighed and weaved his way through the crowd, nodding at every person who murmured, "Hello, Dr. Hart." There was no hiding in a small town.

When Scott got to the gym doors, Adam stopped him. His co-worker grinned and gestured toward the crowd.

"Good turnout," Adam said. "Are you leaving already? Tell me you're not heading in to work."

Scott shook his head and glanced at his watch. He needed to find Rachel before volunteers surrounded her—and before he lost his nerve. "Dr. Smith is covering my call hours. I'm helping Rachel set up for the fun run." *And hopefully making plans for a date tonight*, he thought. "She asked me to show up two hours before the race."

"Let me buy some fifty-fifty tickets, and then I'll meet you outside. I'd like to help, too."

Scott continued through the door, then glanced back into the gym. Adam was chatting with the mom selling tickets. She blushed and fumbled with his change. Then Adam crouched down to talk to a little girl at the ticket table. The girl grinned and nodded, carefully counting out his tickets.

Adam made flirting look easy.

Scott had never considered himself awkward, but Rachel left him all mixed up.

This isn't a big deal, he assured himself. *Just tell her how you feel. Don't complicate things.*

Scott walked toward the race's starting line, looking for Rachel. He found her behind the registration table—surrounded by volunteers. She'd parked her car on the grass, and the trunk was open and filled with boxes of supplies.

So much for catching her alone. Scott brushed off his disappointment and forced a smile on his face. "How can I help?"

"We were about to unload my car. Thanks again for helping with the shirts." Rachel smiled at Scott as she tugged car keys out of her pocket. "Can you move my car once it's empty? I'm going to unbox the shirts on the table."

He nodded and took the keys, then moved the heavy boxes from the car to Rachel's side. Scott squeezed into Rachel's car and searched for a parking spot. To his delight, there was an empty spot near his own Jeep. She was surrounded by people now, but he could wait until she was leaving. Catch her alone. Ask her out to dinner.

Scott rushed back to the registration tables. Volunteers moved in different directions, some with signs in their hands. He didn't recognize many of the faces, so first he stood back and watched the organized chaos. It was just like the emergency room. Everyone had a task, and working together meant every job would get done.

Rachel was pulling the personalized bags of T-shirts and goodies out of their boxes. She worked quickly, even with one good arm. "Do you need a hand?" Scott laughed, surprised by his own joke. "Sorry, not the right choice of words. Can I help you with the shirts?"

Rachel's eyes roamed around the gazebo, assessing what needed to be done. "I can handle the shirts. We're making a balloon arch for the finish line, though. Have you ever worked with balloons?"

He walked over and scanned the kit's instructions. "I can handle this. Point me to the finish line."

Because the one-mile race looped around the school property, the finish line wasn't too far from the start. Scott grabbed the frame first, then a bag of balloons and an electric air pump. Adam joined him shortly afterward. As he filled and tied off each balloon, Scott handed them to his co-worker.

Adam had made plans at the raffle ticket table. He was treating today's volunteers to a dinner after the run and raffle. "I'm helping Emma with cleanup. We'll order food. Have a little celebration after the fundraiser."

Scott hesitated, pinching the balloon shut before tying its end into a knot. "Who's Emma?"

"She's the woman at the ticket table. Blond hair. Cute kid. Mom's cute, too. They both like pizza, so I called in an order for four o'clock."

Scott frowned. He couldn't find a moment alone with Rachel to ask her out, and Adam was organizing lunch with a girl he'd just met. "You hate pizza."

"Hate is a strong word." Adam grinned as he took the balloon and secured it with tape, adding it to the round metal frame. "I ordered subs, too."

The arch was finished, but Scott wasn't done with this conversation. "They're called hoagies here." He hesitated, wondering how to word his advice. "Be careful with Emma. She's got a kid. Are you ready for a commitment like that? Moms don't want men who walk into their life and waltz back out."

Adam raised his eyebrows. "I might take her for coffee. Maybe dinner. That's not a lifelong commitment. Besides, I love kids. I thought I'd have kids of my own by now."

Scott was a few years older than his friend, but understood how Adam felt. Each year, his dream of having a family felt a bit more unreachable. "What happened? Why aren't you married with kids? You're almost out of your twenties." He gave Adam a side eye. "I'm surprised you don't have gray hair yet."

"Life got too busy. I moved from one hospital to the next. With all the moving around, I never found the right woman. Not that I haven't looked." Adam attached the last balloon and stood back to admire his work. "We did a good job. We could sell our skills as balloon artists. The single moms would love us."

Scott wrinkled his nose. "I'm not hunting for moms at birthday parties. That's creepy."

"Easy for you to say. You're dating Rachel."

"We're not dating! I haven't even asked her out," Scott hissed. "Keep your voice down. I'm asking her out tonight."

Adam's face lit up. "Let's bring her over before you chicken out." He raised his voice and waved his arms in the air. "Hey! Rachel! How do the balloons look?"

Scott groaned. "What are you doing?"

"Making sure you see Rachel tonight."

"I don't need help." Scott ground his teeth together. "I've got this."

"Of course you do. And I've got your back."

They stopped talking as Rachel approached them. She walked with a spring in her step, grinning at their finished results. "It looks great! The kids are going to love it."

"Thanks. I'm an expert balloon artist." Adam walked over and gave Rachel a hug. "I'm also a hugger. Good to see you again."

Rachel laughed and gave him a quick squeeze, then turned to face Scott. "Your nurse has hidden talents. He should start twisting animals at work."

Scott joined in the laughter, then shook his head. "Don't give him ideas. Adam's a trouble-maker. He brought in a bubble machine last week. It's all in good fun, though. The kids loved it."

"Speaking of fun!" Adam bounced on the balls of his feet, leaning toward Rachel. "I'm having pizza and subs delivered after the basket raffle is over. Want to join us?"

Scott groaned. Sometimes Adam pushed way too hard. "They're called hoagies. And we might be too tired for a pizza party. I was thinking of a movie and takeout afterward. Your apartment. Just a quiet way to unwind."

"Oh!" Surprise raced across Rachel's face. "The two of us? That sounds like fun, but I'm helping with cleanup. Raincheck for the movie?"

"Sure, no problem." Scott mentally shoved his disappointment into a little box and forced a smile onto his face. "I can stay for cleanup, too. If that's okay."

Adam gave him a thumbs up. Scott just rolled his eyes. *I don't need help finding time with Rachel,* he grumbled to himself. Tomorrow was his last day off work—he'd be working twelve-hour shifts or on-call for the next week. There went his only shot at asking her out for the next few days.

The first runners arrived as they gathered the last of their supplies. Scott was grateful for the distraction. It didn't leave him time to be upset by Adam's intervention.

Still, Rachel hadn't said no to his impromptu movie night. That had to mean something, right?

Scott could be patient. Good things were worth waiting for.

Chapter Twenty-One

Rachel

"Three...two...one... Go!" Rachel yelled, officially starting the fun run.

Nearly two hundred kids surged forward from the starting line, many of their faces decorated with a rainbow, butterfly, or the Sunset Elementary mascot. Their face-painting booth had been a hit.

Tears stung her eyes as the students surged past her. The entire community had come out to help the hospital today. Their kids were running, they were buying baked goods, or they'd bought tickets for the basket raffle. Everyone was involved in some way.

This was small-town living at its best. Rachel felt another wave of gratitude for the residents of Sunset Cove. She couldn't imagine living in a better place.

This was her home, and these were her kids. As busy as her schedule was, she was glad she'd taken on raising money for a new pediatric ward.

Besides, the fundraisers had brought her closer to Scott. Rachel thought about the handsome doctor as she walked toward the finish line, where many of the parents and spectators waited. Scott had been an unexpected find in Sunset Cove. She'd never felt this way about a man before.

She hadn't expected Scott to invite himself over for dinner and a movie. It was tempting, but Rachel couldn't abandon her friends during cleanup. She hoped he didn't mind the rain check.

Rachel found a spot near the finish line next to Harry. As expected, he was standing at the front of the pack, cheering on his granddaughters as they raced the mile around the school's athletic fields.

"You've got some fast kids here today," Harry commented. "The oldest ones are halfway done."

"There's a growth spurt in late elementary school," Scott chimed in, easing up to Rachel's side. "Longer legs, bigger lung capacity. Wait until these kids get older. They're fast now, but they'll fly across the track in high school."

Rachel chuckled. It must be interesting to view the world from a doctor's perspective.

The crowd cheered as kids approached the finish line. To her delight, Emily Wilde was the first to finish. She raised her hands in the hair, pumping her arms as she broke through the paper ribbon.

Scott stepped forward and handed her a cup of water. "Drink up. Nice job running today."

Emily grinned and accepted the drink. Though her face was already pink from running, she blushed a deeper shade of red as she looked at the attractive doctor.

"You were at the hospital," she blurted out. "When our bus crashed."

Scott nodded. "That's right. I'm a doctor. I hope you stay healthy and I don't see you too often." When she continued staring at him, he gestured toward the cup of water. "Drink. It's hot today. You don't want to get dehydrated."

Emily bobbed her head and took a few sips of water.

Rachel bit back a grin. Brook had a point when she called him Hot Scott. Even preteens were struck speechless. She grinned and wondered if it helped or hurt to be such a handsome doctor.

Dozens of children crossed the finish line, and Rachel was soon scrambling alongside her volunteers to make sure every child had water. She urged the finishers to find their parents and wait in the shade. They wouldn't be outside much longer with this heat.

Rachel grabbed the microphone and stood next to the portable loudspeaker to address the crowd. "Thank you so much for coming today! I hope you all had fun."

She waited as the crowd cheered, grinning as the children hopped up and down in their colorful race shirts. "As you know, today's fundraiser is for the local hospital. They're building a new children's ward. It's our hope that one day soon, no child in Sunset Cove will have to travel for medical care. Thanks to you, we're one step closer to making that happen."

Rachel swallowed another lump in her throat as her eyes scanned over the crowd, spying Aubrey O'Grady with her parents. Aubrey looked so healthy now. Her hair was growing back, and she was strong enough to run a mile. Modern medicine was amazing.

Scott seemed to sense her overwhelm. He stepped forward and touched her shoulder. "Do you need a minute?" he murmured. When she nodded, he took the microphone.

"My name is Dr. Scott Hart. I'm the head emergency room pediatrician. Some of you have had the unfortunate experience of meeting me at the hospital." He paused for a moment as the crowd chuckled. "I've lived in many towns over the years, and this is one of the most close-knit communities I've experienced. Thank you for supporting our hospital. We're going to do amazing things for your children. If they need medical care, we'll be ready and waiting for them." He paused again, scanning the crowd and making eye contact with the children. "Wear your seat belt. Get a bike helmet. And don't forget to use sunscreen."

The parents laughed as Scott handed the microphone back to Rachel. She laughed as well, amazed at Scott's ability to energize a crowd. He'd also given her the time she needed to pull back her emotions and finish her job.

She announced the top three winners in each age division, handing every winner a medal and gift certificate for one treat at Seaside Cupcakes. Brook had donated the certificates. While Brook didn't run, she believed any kid who would run to raise money deserved a cupcake or brownie, at the very least.

The crowd dispersed once they'd handed out the last awards. Kids and parents went home or inside to check out the basket raffle. She'd seen lots of parents carrying bags from the bake sale. Rachel was thrilled. The run itself had raised over two thousand dollars.

Sure, they'd only raised the equivalent of a few gala tickets. But every dollar mattered when you had a large project.

Scott and Adam stayed behind to clean up after the race.

Adam stood in front of the balloon arch and grimaced. "Do we have to pop it? It would look awesome at work. I hate to destroy this a few hours after putting it together."

Rachel put her hand on her hip and sized up the arch. Would it fit in a pickup truck? "Don't pop it yet. I'll ask Grant if he can move it. He owns a construction company. If anyone's got the equipment to move it, it's him."

Scott nodded. "Grant's in charge of the hospital project, remember? Ask him if he can move it. The kids would enjoy it."

With that taken care of, they emptied trash cans and dragged garbage to the school dumpster. Scott gathered empty boxes for recycling and packed up the materials left after the race. When they were done, he put the supplies in her trunk. "Should we go inside? It's almost time to pick the basket raffle winners."

Rachel's face lit up. "I want to win the box of art supplies. I have a few kids who love drawing in my room."

"Aren't you a music teacher?" Adam cocked his head in confusion.

"I am, but sometimes kids have free time and hang out in my room. They don't always want to play the xylophones. Sometimes they want to draw, and that's fine. Art is art. My room is a safe space."

"That's the perfect answer," Adam replied, looking impressed. "I hope you win the art supplies. Maybe Scott can find you a summer job in our Child Life department."

"We don't have a Child Life department yet," Scott replied. "I'm sure Rachel enjoys having summers off."

"I'm working at the bakery this summer," she admitted. "What's Child Life?"

"They work with kids who are scared or bored. Try to distract them while they're in the hospital," Adam said. "We don't have a Child Life department now, but it's on Scott's wish list."

Rachel's eyes lit up. "It's a wonderful idea. I hope you find the money to make it happen."

Inside the gym, drawings for the basket raffle drawings had begun. Things moved quickly, with Harry pulling out a ticket for every prize and Pastor Rick announcing the lucky winner. Rachel was disappointed that she hadn't won the art supplies, but she cheered when Scott won the sunrise boat ride.

Scott grinned sheepishly as he accepted his prize. He walked back to Rachel, freeing the dolphin from its cling wrap and handing it to her. "I hear you like the ocean. Have you ever been on the dolphin-watching boat?"

Rachel shook her head. "It's been years since I went on the tour. Silly, right? I'm off school all summer. I hope you have fun, though. It sounds amazing."

"It's breakfast for two," he said, shrugging his shoulders. "I'm supposed to share the prize with someone."

Rachel's face flushed. "Unless you're hungry enough to eat breakfast for two, I suppose." She turned her focus back to Pastor Rick, who was announcing the rest of the winners.

Nick's daughters won the baking lessons at Seaside Cupcakes. The girls cheered and ran to the pastor to accept their prize.

Rachel smiled and clapped for the girls, but her mind spun over Scott's words. Was he inviting her out to breakfast? And why had he asked to do dinner and a movie tonight? She'd need to steel her heart against hurt if he wasn't serious about dating her. It was too soon to get her hopes up.

She continued to think about Scott's words as the raffle wrapped up and people left the room. To her surprise, Scott remained by her side.

"Should we clean up?" he asked. "Adam says the pizza should be here soon."

Rachel nodded and walked toward the remnants of the basket raffle, pulling off each table covering and tossing it into a laundry basket for the Kindness Committee's next event.

"Let me help," Scott said, grabbing the basket she was balancing on one hip. He followed her around the room, helping her gather each tablecloth in the basket.

Once they had cleared the tables, Rachel looked around the room. The team was done clearing the gym—and just in time. A man from Joey's pizza walked through the door with a stack of pizzas and salads.

Adam followed behind him with a grin, carrying a box of foil-wrapped hoagies. "Let's eat! You've all got to be hungry."

Rachel sat at a cafeteria table with her friends. She sighed as she lounged in the chair, resting her cast and sling on the table. It felt wonderful to rest. Time to relax and let go of her worries about Scott for a few minutes.

"Don't look now, but I think the doctor's headed our way," Emma whispered. "I think he likes you."

Avery covered her mouth and laughed. "Of course he likes Rachel. But have you seen the way Adam looks at you, Emma? Someone else has a crush."

Emma blushed and shook her head, looking around to make sure her daughter couldn't hear the conversation. "I'm ready to date again, but Adam seems a little young."

"He's three years older than you," Brook volunteered. "We talked about high school graduation years. Besides, he's perfect for you. He's only met your daughter once and she can't stop talking about him. He likes kids, and they like him. That's important."

"Who do we like?" Kendra asked, bouncing toward her mom's table with a slice of pizza.

"We like everybody," Emma said warily, shooting daggers at her friend.

Scott walked up to the table, carrying food and dragging a chair behind him. He slid the seat next to Rachel and smiled at the young girl. "I like everybody here, too. Don't you, Kendra?"

"We moved here when I was a baby. The people are nice." Kendra grinned and took a bite of pizza, then leaded toward Avery's daughter and started giggling, clearly sharing an inside joke.

Rachel sat back and watched her friends and their children, soaking it all in. This was Sunset Cove at its best—friends working together, building a better life for everyone in town.

Her mood stayed high as Adam joined them, dragging his own chair. The rest of her friends shifted closer to make space. Rachel could feel the heat radiating off Scott's body now.

Instead of shifting away, she smiled at Scott. Being this close felt comfortable. Safe. Despite spending hours in the scorching sun, he smelled nice, too—a deep, musky scent. Rachel fought off the urge to snuggle closer.

She sat up straighter and grabbed a piece of pizza off her plate. What was she thinking? She couldn't snuggle up to Scott. They were friends. He'd asked to do dinner and a movie tonight, but that didn't mean he was interested in her.

The rest of the table seemed oblivious to her growing confusion. Conversation continued to flow around her, new and old friends' voices mixing with laughter.

Adam was in the best mood out of everyone. "I love the people in this town," he announced. "What about you, Scott? I can see us staying in Sunset Cove for a long time." His face broke into a grin as he glanced around the girls' table, focusing most of his attention on Emma. "I'm tired of moving from one hospital to the next. It's time to stick to one place."

Rachel's eyes drifted toward Brooke, who smirked behind her napkin as Scott shifted in his seat, glaring at Adam. What was that supposed to mean?

Chapter Twenty-Two

Scott

Scott paced around his kitchen, wiping off counters and straightening paperwork that needed to be reviewed.

He scrambled some eggs and ate breakfast, then wiped the counters down again and washed his dishes by hand. His older, Victorian-style home had a modern kitchen and dishwasher, but he didn't use it. Washing plates and cups was his new way of unwinding and burning off excess energy.

Scott felt filled with nervous energy. It was his last day off work for a week, and he couldn't settle down to get anything done.

He'd tried to fix the leaky sink in his bathroom. Instead, he'd made the leak worse. A plumber was coming this afternoon.

He'd glanced through the latest edition of *Pediatric Care Today*, but couldn't focus enough to read the articles.

Scott had even tried turning on television, hoping to take his mind off Rachel.

None of it worked. No matter what he did, Scott couldn't stop thinking about the woman who had captured his heart.

He wondered what she was doing, and if she'd recovered from the weekend's race. Scott glanced at his phone. He could just text her, or call. Did guys still call girls they wanted to date?

Scott tucked his phone back into his jeans pocket and chuckled. What was he thinking? He liked Rachel, but she needed some space. He'd already invited her to watch a movie, and go out to breakfast on the dolphin-watching boat. She hadn't seemed too interested in either prospect. At least, she hadn't said "yes."

She hadn't said "no," either. He wouldn't lose hope yet.

Scott sighed and flipped through the television channels one last time. Rachel was right to hesitate. When he found a woman to care about, he wanted it all—a wife, children, and time to spend with his family. Other doctors had found that balance. But for now, he was the only pediatric doctor in a small-town emergency room. It wasn't a great time to date someone new.

You won't be the only pediatric doctor for long, he reminded himself. *You'll have a more reasonable schedule soon.* Once they hired a few more physicians, he could turn his focus to the new pediatric wing. That meant a more regular schedule. Steady hours. Less on-call days.

Scott threw down the television remote. What was he waiting for? Nick was right. He needed to keep showing up. Tell Rachel he was interested, until she said "yes" or turned him down for real. He yanked the phone out of his pocket and opened his texting app.

> What time's your lunch break?

Rachel
> 11:15
>
> Why?

Scott checked the clock and grinned. Her break didn't start for another thirty minutes.

> Want some company?

Twenty-five minutes later, he stood outside Sunset Cove Elementary School with a box from Seaside Cupcakes. The best bakery in town sold sandwiches now—how convenient was that? His stomach growled as he thought about the Italian hoagie and warm cookies waiting for him inside the lunch box.

The school secretary buzzed him in. He lingered in the office as minutes passed by. Scott could be patient. He'd waited a lifetime to find a woman like Rachel. He could wait five more minutes until her break started.

Scott was eyeing up his boxed lunch, trying to decide if he could sneak a cookie, when Allen walked into the office.

"Hello! Can I help you with anything?" the principal asked.

Scott shook his head. "I'm just waiting for Rachel. Ms. Lancaster," he corrected himself. "I brought her some lunch."

The principal glanced at Scott's name badge, which sported his first and last name alongside a photograph. "Scott Hart. Are you Dr. Hart, the new head of pediatrics?"

"I am."

Allen held out his hand and smiled, his face lighting up in genuine warmth. "I'm Allen Sawyer, the school principal. I'd hoped to see you at the fundraiser, but my kid's baseball game ran into extra innings. It's a pleasure to meet you. Rachel speaks highly of you."

Scott reached out and offered a firm handshake. "Thank you, sir. Rachel's been a lot of help. They raised a lot of money this weekend for the hospital, and she's putting some songs together for our larger fundraiser, too."

"The children's choir." Allen brightened as he sat down next to Scott. "She's got a talented group of kids. I'm impressed with Rachel's work this year. Even a broken arm couldn't hold her back."

Scott nodded. "I haven't heard the choir yet, but she'll do a great job. Rachel's pretty special." He cleared his throat and stared down at his boxed lunch, wondering if he'd revealed too much. After all, this was the principal of Rachel's school. Scott didn't understand the hierarchy of school employees, and he didn't want to cause any problems.

The two men sat in silence, letting the awkward tension build. Then Allen stood up and patted Scott on the shoulder. "She's special, all right. I've been working with Rachel since she moved to Sunset Cove. First as a teacher, now as her principal. There's something different about her this year. She seems happier. More fulfilled. That surprised me, because I thought she had too much on her plate. Between the gala's choir and her own fundraiser, she's been busy."

Allen paused, crossing his arms as he squared himself in front of Scott's chair. "I'm an administrator at this school, but I'm also Rachel's friend. The choir cheered her up, but I suspect her newfound happiness has more to do with you." He looked Scott in the eyes. "Don't hurt her. Don't start something if you can't commit."

Scott furrowed his brows as he considered Allen's words. He'd fallen hard for Rachel. Rachel seemed to like him, too. But their crazy schedules kept pulling them apart. Even if he started working fewer hours, she'd still be dedicated to her students.

Allen nodded and glanced at the clock. "I've given you enough to think about. I'll head back to my office now. Rachel should be here any minute."

Scott drummed his fingers on the arm of the chair, now impatient as a line of children marched past the office windows and toward the cafeteria. A few children peered into the office and waved. Then three adults walked past Scott, giving him curious glances as they entered the mailroom.

Finally, Rachel rushed into the office. "Almost ready," she said over her shoulder, handing the office secretary a stack of papers. "These are for Allen and the school board members. They asked for a final tally from the fun run and basket raffle."

She walked over to Scott and let out a huff of breath. "Sorry, it's been a busy day. I emailed you this morning, after Pastor Rick made our bank deposit. We raised over thirty thousand dollars!"

His eyes widened. Scott had seen the number of kids running and the people milling around the basket raffle. He had suspected the fundraiser was a huge success—but Rachel still managed to surprise him.

Scott didn't check his email on days off, but he would make an exception after lunch. "That's incredible. You deserve to celebrate the success." He held up the boxed lunch. "Cookies?"

Rachel grinned and eyed the box in his hands. "Are those Brook's cookies?"

"Double chocolate chunk, still warm from the oven," he replied. "It's not rocky road ice cream, but it's as close as I could get."

"It's a good choice," she assured Scott, leading him down the hall to her classroom. "I've got thirty-three minutes left in my lunch break. Don't mind the mess," she said, pushing the door open. "School ends in a week, and I'm having trouble packing up with just one arm. I'm making more of a mess than usual."

Scott glanced around the classroom, taking in the details and looking past the mess. He loved school and had a huge respect for teachers, but he'd never considered the time and dedication they put into their job.

Stacks of papers, a pile of recorders, and a teetering tower of folders lined her windowsill. Rachel sighed and gestured toward the window. "If you're bored, I have twenty recorders to sanitize. They're from the kids who couldn't afford to buy their own. The last one came back today."

Scott nodded. It didn't surprise him that Sunset Cove Elementary School had its share of lower-income students. The town was filled with costly houses, but there were enough parents struggling to pay their bills on the outskirts of town. One of his goals was to establish a medical trust fund for families who couldn't afford care. At this rate, he'd have enough projects to stay busy for a long time. "We'll eat fast and sanitize when we're done eating. I'm happy to help."

Scott dragged two chairs together and gestured for Rachel to sit down, then opened the foil-wrapped cookies and set them on a chair between them. His stomach got the best of him, and he unwrapped his sandwich to take a hearty bite.

Scott held back a sigh. Why was this town's food so good? It was like Brook sprinkled everything with fairy dust to keep the tourists coming back.

Rachel tore open a bag with one hand and pulled out half of a sandwich. She reached out to add a cookie to her meal. "Thanks for the treat. The last week of school drags by. But why are you here? Not that I hate spending time with you, of course."

Scott brightened at the comment. "I thought you'd like cookies. And I like spending time with you, too. Do I need another reason?"

"Nope." She laughed and bit into the cookie, then brushed the crumbs off her face. "Cookies are an excellent reason to visit, especially the last week of school."

"I thought you'd be excited to finish school."

"I am. But the kids are excited, too. It's hard to keep them focused. The year will be over soon enough. Then I'll have the entire summer to recuperate—when I'm not working in Brook's bakery."

He raised an eyebrow. "You mentioned something on Saturday. You're working at the bakery this summer?"

"She needs the help." Rachel shrugged. "Brook's lunch menu was a hit. Avery can't work more hours, and her baby will be here soon. I'm filling the gaps while Brook trains a teenager to help her."

"Sounds like a busy summer." Scott frowned at his sandwich before taking another bite. As he chewed, he thought about Rachel's schedule. Between both of their commitments, they'd never find time to be together. "You'll have choir practice, too?"

She nodded and took a sip of water. "Once a week, until the gala happens. It'll be nice to see the students over the summer. I miss them over break."

Scott smiled, loving the way she enjoyed her students. "At least you don't view it as work." He glanced around the room again, taking in the piles of papers and half-filled boxes. "I don't know how you'll pack up by next week, though."

"The art teacher stops by every day. She carries a box to my car. We'll get it done."

"She's got her own classroom to clean up, though." Scott cocked his head. "What's your deadline? When do you need to be done?"

"Next year's supplies can stay here, but I need things at home to plan lessons for the fall. We have until next Wednesday to pack up. Then the janitors take over and clean every classroom."

Scott nodded and took another bite of his sandwich, then opened the scheduling app on his phone. "I have off Tuesday and Wednesday. Can I help you pack?"

"I'd appreciate that. My friends work during the day, so I'd be grateful for any help. Are you sure, though? You need days off, too."

He nodded, glad for another excuse to spend time together. Scott crumbled his sandwich wrapper and threw it back into the lunch box. "I'm happy to help. Besides, I don't hate spending time with you, either."

The quip earned him a hearty laugh.

They wrapped up lunch and moved on to washing the recorders. As Scott swished the instruments in warm, soapy water, he turned to smile at Rachel. "I've still got a breakfast boat ride to share, you know. There might be dolphins." He hesitated, watching as the confusion grew on Rachel's face. "I'd like to take you with me. If you're interested."

Surprise replaced the confusion. Rachel took her time drying the recorder, carefully pulling a strand of cotton through the barrel before making eye contact with him. "I'd love to go." She bit her lip and hesitated. "It's the start of tourist season, though. I promised Brook I'd work mornings and afternoons, remember? Tourist season winds down in late August. I can take a morning or two off after the gala."

Disappointment settled in Scott's gut, but did his best to ignore it. Rachel hadn't said "no." She'd only said "not yet." He nodded and smiled. "I'll call the boat owner and ask about dates after the gala. And I'll text you next week to confirm a time to clean out your classroom."

He left the school a few minutes later, feeling like he'd failed at capturing Rachel's interest. This was the second time she'd given him a raincheck. But despite his frustration, Scott knew he couldn't walk away. They were both busy—but life was busy. It was only a matter of time before she agreed to go on a date.

Maybe Nick was right. Rachel wouldn't pay attention to subtle hints. He'd have to set himself squarely in front of her. After the gala, it was time to make his intentions clear. He was falling in love with Rachel Lancaster.

Scott sent up a prayer that Rachel would soon feel the same way.

Chapter Twenty-Three

Rachel

THE WEEK FLEW BY, as the last week of school often did.

Excited students filled Rachel's classroom, and the days blurred into a rush of last-minute lessons and fun. The days were long, but they stacked together quickly. Then it was time to say goodbye for the summer.

Rachel was grateful to live in a small town, where it wasn't uncommon to run into students at the library or grocery store. That didn't happen in Michigan.

As promised, Scott had texted and scheduled a time to pack. They met at eight o'clock, joining the line of sleepy-eyed teachers walking into the building to clean their classrooms before next year.

"This is the first day of summer break?" Scott asked, looking around the parking lot. There were more cars here than usual—lots of teachers brought their spouses and friends to help. Now that the students were gone, the doors were unlocked and propped open. No security guards or sign-in sheets in sight.

"This is how teachers start their summer," she confirmed, carrying an empty box with one arm. The orthopedist was confident the cast could come off soon. Rachel was eager to get the heavy, itchy weight off her arm, even if she was stuck in a sling. "Ready to pack? My room is still a mess."

Scott shrugged and juggled his own boxes as they walked down the hall. "It's no worse than the emergency room after a bad day. You focus on what matters. That's the kids, while they're here. Now that they're gone, you can focus on cleaning up."

"I like that attitude." She smiled as she opened the classroom door. "The kids are my top priority. But the room..." Rachel groaned as Scott peeked inside. "I'm really, really sorry. And grateful for the help."

Scott's eyes widened as he took in the mess. Rachel tried to view the room from his perspective. The neat stacks from last week had multiplied. She had flung open her cabinet doors, showcasing shelves that were either empty or filled to overflowing. It was enough to send a weaker man running.

Fortunately, Scott wasn't weak. He put his hand on her back, sending shivers down her spine as he guided her forward. "Looks like we've got a solid day's work ahead of us. Where should I start?"

Rachel spent the next few hours directing Scott's efforts and packing boxes with one arm. More than once, she stopped to reflect on their progress. They'd sorted through all of her cabinets, repacking what needed to stay and pulling out the lesson materials for next year. A box of supplies sat near the door, waiting to be packed into her car.

She also took a few chances, when he wasn't looking, to admire Scott's muscles in his short-sleeve shirt. He often stuck to button-down shirts, and she'd seen him in a doctor's white coat more than once. He looked different in a T-shirt. More approachable. More appealing.

Not that he wasn't appealing before, Rachel reminded herself. *He's a nice guy. I don't like him just because of his muscles.*

They stopped for lunch when the principal delivered slices of pizza. Then Scott and Rachel kept working, slowly but steadily straightening up the classroom.

At four o'clock, the principal announced that it was time to lock the building. Rachel glanced up in surprise. Filled boxes lined the hallway, and they were nearly done packing up her room. "I'd never get this done alone," she admitted. "Thank you again."

Scott looked pleased. "It's no problem. I'm glad I could help. Should we get these boxes down to your car?"

She nodded, looping a canvas bag over her shoulder. Rachel couldn't carry boxes, but that didn't mean she couldn't move things outside. Together, they emptied the hallway and filled her car, then tucked a few more boxes into Scott's Jeep.

Scott followed Rachel back to her apartment. Despite the long day, he was having a good time. Rachel laughed as she glanced in her rearview mirror. Scott was singing along to the radio, bopping his head to the beat. He wasn't just attractive. He was adorable, and a great guy to be around.

What would she do about Scott? He'd asked her out twice, and each time she'd claimed to be too busy.

Rachel *was* busy. She crashed into bed late each night, exhausted. Things would be easier now that school was over, but she'd still be working at Brook's bakery and practicing with the children's choir.

She'd need to make a choice soon: Admit her attraction to Scott and find time to date, or commit to staying single.

Rachel's life would always be filled with children, but this could be her only chance to build a life with someone.

Did it make her selfish to want Scott in her world? This amazing man deserved more than she could offer, but the thought of letting him go made her heart hurt.

·♥·♥·♥·♥·♥·

Rachel's thoughts spun with indecision as Scott parked on the curb next to her apartment.

Scott grabbed the first box of classroom supplies from her trunk and grinned, then gestured toward the building. "Ladies first. Can you unlock the door?"

They made multiple trips from the car to her apartment, moving boxes and bags until Rachel's trunk was empty. She looked around her home in amazement. They'd stacked supplies in the living room, where she could sort them over the summer. Scott had saved Rachel and her friends hours of work.

Her stomach rumbled, reminding her that they'd only had a slice of pizza today. "Thanks again. I'm not cooking much with one arm, but can I offer you a sandwich? Brook keeps my fridge stocked with easy meals."

Rachel held her breath, hoping he would stay. She still wasn't sure how their relationship could work, but she enjoyed spending time with Scott.

To her disappointment, he shook his head. "Thanks, but I've got a business dinner with the hospital CEO. We're meeting to finalize the gala plans, and go through some last-minute expansion changes. Construction's moving faster than we planned, thanks to extra donations." Scott nodded at Rachel. "The school played a big role in that. You did, too."

Rachel's face flushed. She was glad the school's efforts had helped so much, but all she could imagine was Scott sitting in a fancy restaurant, his arm stretched over the white tablecloth, touching another woman's hand. Jealousy flooded her mind as she pictured the tall blonde from their construction site tour.

This was her fault. If she'd showed more interest, Rachel wouldn't be worried about Scott dating other women. Now it was too late. He'd gotten bored with her games and busy schedule.

But if he had plans with the CEO, why had he asked her out again? She swallowed her pride and tried to find the information she needed. "That's great. I hope you have a nice dinner with her."

Scott blinked, looking confused. "Her? No, the CEO is William Stewart. You met him during our tour of the new wing." He chuckled, shaking his head. "His wife will probably join us, though. She's very involved at the hospital. She reminds me of you."

Rachel felt a surge of relief, and a bit of embarrassment. "Sorry. I thought..."

Understanding dawned in Scott's eyes. "I'm just glad the trustees aren't joining us. Michelle was at the tour, too. She's our newest trustee. Tall, blond. I'm not sure I'd enjoy dinner with her. She's not my type."

This is awkward, Rachel thought. *I shouldn't have asked about dinner. But if he isn't interested in Michelle...*

She took a deep breath. If she didn't speak up now, she might never have the chance—or the courage. "Would you go to dinner with me? I promise that I'm not tall. Or blond." Rachel tried to soften the joke with a smile, hiding her nerves behind the grin.

Scott's eyes widened for a moment. He nodded and reached out to touch her hand. "I thought you'd never ask. I work nights this week, but my mornings are open. What do you say to breakfast?" He tugged his phone out of his jeans pocket and opened his schedule. "If you're still interested in the dolphin tour, we could do a sunrise breakfast next week. If the boat's available, of course."

Rachel mentally reviewed her own schedule and decided that Brook would want her to take this chance. She'd work earlier and get the baking done before dawn. "Sounds like a plan."

"I'm not rushing out the door, but I need to get ready for my meeting," Scott said, twisting his face in a frown before squeezing her hand again. "I'll see you tomorrow morning? My shift starts at noon, but I can help you finish packing."

Rachel smiled as he walked out the door, leaving her alone—but a lot less lonely than normal.

This felt like the start of something special.

Chapter Twenty-Four

Scott

SCOTT PARKED IN FRONT of the school, more confident and cheerful than the day before.

Rachel was finally on the same page. They were going on a date, and he couldn't be more excited.

He'd already called the tour boat company. They couldn't take their breakfast cruise for a few weeks, but that was fine. They would go after the gala was over, when they could both relax and celebrate their success.

His meeting with the CEO had gone well, too. The hospital would contact Dr. Sonya Epstein this week and offer her a position in the emergency room. Their offer would be generous—more money than she currently earned, and a chance to fill Scott's role as head of emergency care. Scott would shift his focus from the ER to the new pediatric wing.

If Sonya accepted their offer, it could mean Scott would have more free time, and soon.

He whistled as he got out of the car and walked toward the school. He sat on a bench to wait for Rachel. Scott needed to work later today, but knew they would finish the job in time. If he worked smart, they might have time for an early lunch.

Yes, there were lots of reasons to be cheerful today.

Scott grinned and waved as Rachel parked in front of the school and walked toward him. She was beautiful, kind, and intelligent.

He bowed his head and gave thanks for having Rachel in his life, and prayed that things would work out between them.

When he opened his eyes, a man in baggy jeans and a white tank top was strolling toward Rachel. Scott shot up from the bench, observing the man. Maybe he was Rachel's friend. But every instinct he'd developed on the job said trouble was brewing.

Scott watched with concern as Cory Wilde grabbed Rachel's good arm, causing her to nearly lose her balance.

Time to act. No one touched his friends—especially Rachel—like that. "Hey, man," he called, moving toward the two of them. "What's going on?"

The man ignored Scott. "You stupid little girl," he hissed. "I lost custody of my kid because of you."

Rachel had gone white with fear. She looked around for help, her face tight as she made eye contact Scott. The tears in her eyes sent a surge of anger through Scott. He rushed forward and tried to wedge himself between the man and Rachel.

"Get your hands off her," Scott said, working to keep his voice steady.

"Make me."

Rachel tugged her arm, her voice shaking when she couldn't pull free. "Mr. Wilde, please let me go. I'm very sorry about Emma, but we can talk about this inside. In the office. Like reasonable adults."

"I'll show you what reasonable adults do," he replied, dragging her a few feet away from the school. "You cost me my kid, and now some judge says I owe child support. You're gonna pay for this."

Enough talking, Scott decided. He wrapped both arms around Rachel's waist and pulled her out of Cory's grasp, then pushed Rachel behind him. "It's time for you to leave. Judges don't look kindly on parents who commit assault. Don't do anything you might regret."

Scott noticed a flurry of activity coming from the school building. He ignored it, keeping his focus on the angry man in front of him.

Rachel took a steadying breath, letting it out slowly. "The principal's coming out."

Scott nodded, but didn't shift his attention from the threat. He wouldn't drop his guard until this man was far away from Rachel.

Principal Sawyer stepped between the two men. "Cory Wilde. It's a pleasure to see you again, although you don't have permission to be on school property. How can I help you today?"

"This... teacher," he spit out the word, clearly wanting to call Rachel something worse. "She must've contacted the county. Child protective services helped my wife get custody of my kid. Do you know how expensive child support is? Your teacher cost me a ton of money. She needs to pay up."

Scott's stomach twisted in disgust. This guy lost custody of his kid, and he was coming after Rachel for money? His vision flashed red with rage. He'd never punched someone before. But if there was going to be a time, it might be today.

Scott took a breath and tried to calm down. No use getting charged with assault alongside this so-called father. Scott's focus needed to stay on Rachel. He'd do almost anything to keep her safe.

This new urge to protect Rachel surprised him. He'd never felt this way before.

"Ms. Lancaster didn't contact the county. I did," the principal offered. "I shared the footage of you dragging her toward your car. We're being recorded today, too. You need to leave."

Allen stayed silent, waiting for Cory's next move.

To Scott's relief, Cory took a step backward. He gave Rachel one last look of hatred and continued backing away. "This isn't over. This is your fault!"

The two educators stood with Scott until Cory slammed his car door and drove away, tires squealing. Allen frowned at Scott and Rachel. "Let's call the police. It might be time to consider a restraining order."

Scott nodded, placing his hand on Rachel's back as they walked into the building together. He'd meant his touch to be flirtatious yesterday. Today, he was offering comfort and support. Scott hoped she could tell the difference.

Rachel gave Scott a grim smile. "That was Cory Wilde. He's one of my student's parents, and tried to drag me into his car on school property. I guess a few other things happened at home. He lost custody of his daughter. Mom said he was furious."

"He's not allowed on school property," Allen added. "Mom removed him from the approved pick-up list."

Scott's jaw tightened. "He must be a wonderful father. I've seen a lot of horror stories, but I've never been so close to witnessing an assault."

The principal sighed and nodded. "Sunset Cove is a friendly town. Things like this don't happen often. Mr. Wilde is limited to supervised visitation. He's looking for someone to blame."

Scott felt another surge of anger as Rachel rubbed her arm. A bruise was forming where Cory had grabbed her. "He can start by looking in the mirror. I should get Rachel to the hospital. Or the police station. We need to file charges."

"Why don't the police come here?" the principal suggested. "They can view the surveillance footage and take our statements. In the meantime, take a breather. Finish cleaning out your classroom."

Scott and Rachel walked down the hallway in silence. Rachel hesitated at the doorway. Her room was nearly empty, with just a few piles left to pack up. "There's not much to do. I'm tempted to stuff things into the closet and deal with it next year."

But Scott shook his head. "Today's the last chance to clean, right? It shouldn't take long. You'll feel better with a fresh start next year."

Rachel hesitated, then nodded. They worked side by side, both reluctant to work across the room from the other. They stood close enough together that Rachel bumped into him when the phone rang, making her jump in surprise.

The police had arrived. They walked down to the main office to leave statements. Rachel allowed the police to take pictures of her bruised arm. By the time they were done, she looked exhausted.

Scott rubbed his face as they walked back to her classroom one last time. "I don't enjoy being a mandated reporter."

"What do you mean?"

"Doctors have to report abuse, or even suspected abuse. Just like teachers." He walked to the windows lining Rachel's classroom and stared out at the playground. "I used to think I would keep kids out of these situations. Notice the signs, make sure they get help. It's not that easy in real life." He turned to look at Rachel. "I can't stop people from getting hurt. Sometimes it's kids. Sometimes it's an adult. But it's always hard to watch."

Rachel sighed and walked over to the window. She leaned into Scott's chest, letting him wrap an arm around her. She fit perfectly, like she belonged there, he noted.

"It's tough," she agreed. "But I'll never stop fighting for my students. They deserve to have someone fighting for them." Rachel twisted to look up at Scott. "That man's daughter is in the choir. She's a fantastic singer, and one of the most cheerful students in my class. It's still hard to believe her home life is so tough."

Scott rubbed a hand over her back and nodded. "She's safe for now, and that's what matters. It sounds like the police are going to press charges this time. The judge might even approve a restraining order against her dad."

"It will work out." Rachel sighed and leaned into Scott again. "At least she'll have a few more weeks of fun at choir practice."

Scott nodded, then nudged her away. "Music cures a lot of problems. Let's move these boxes to your car. You deserve to relax the rest of today."

Chapter Twenty-Five

Rachel

RACHEL'S EYES WIDENED WITH surprise as she walked through the lobby of Golden Tides.

It had been two weeks since they'd finished clearing out her classroom. They still hadn't found time for that first date, but Rachel hoped it would happen after the gala.

With just one day left until the fundraiser, they were doing a final walk-through of the ballroom today. It was their last chance to get the space ready for its guests and performers.

Scott beamed at the velvet rope and red carpet that would lead their supporters to the ballroom. "What do you think?"

"It's very elegant." She stopped on the carpet, her eyes sweeping over golden balloons and statues that guarded the entryway. "Is that an Oscar Award?"

He nodded. "The theme is 'Hollywood.' You're using songs from pop culture and award-winning movies, so it seemed like a good fit."

She laughed and reached out to touch an oversized Oscar, then stopped herself. The statues were golden and nearly five feet tall. It was an impressive addition to the understated doorway.

"Come inside. There's so much more to see." Scott reached for her hand and tugged her into the ballroom. A grin stretched across his face. He looked less like a prestigious doctor, and more like an excited kid on Christmas.

Rachel smiled back at him, a familiar mix of attraction and admiration making her stomach twist in knots. Scott was a great guy. They'd seen each other often while working on the gala. Would that change after the fundraiser was over?

She knew things would be different, but wished they didn't have to change. Rachel would miss seeing Scott so often.

Rachel let out a sigh of delight as she entered the ballroom. It was an exquisitely decorated room, but Scott's team had turned the space into something even more amazing.

Sheer golden curtains had replaced the dark, heavy window treatments, bringing in more light and creating a shimmery glow through the room.

A trail of oversized stars was scattered across the floor and in front of the buffet tables. Like the Hollywood Walk of Fame, each star featured the name of a person or business. "They're temporary, of course," Scott offered. "We'll have permanent stars inside the hospital. These are some of our biggest sponsors. A ticket gets you in the door, but an extra ten grand earns you a golden star."

Ten thousand dollars for a star on the floor? Rachel's heart pounded as she eyed up the line of stars in front of them, creating a path across the dance floor and out to the courtyard. "There's at least forty or fifty stars. That's a lot of money."

Scott nodded. "Our 'walk of fame' campaign raised a half-million dollars on its own. I've got you to thank, too. We picked a Hollywood theme after you chose such great songs." He squeezed her hand again, then spun her toward the side of the room. They'd agreed that the far wall was a good place for the string quartet and children's choir. "What do you think of the stage?"

Rachel gasped as she took in the performance area. They'd brought in plain white bleachers, but added gold and black sculptures to make it look like an old-fashioned movie film was twisting up the side of the risers. Rising above the bleachers was an enormous balloon arch, filled with sparkly gold and white balloons. "It's even better than I imagined. Was this all your idea?"

"The hotel has a decorating team. We met with them and came up with some concepts together." Scott grinned and gestured at the arch. "The balloons were my idea. Fortunately, we hired someone to blow them up this time. One balloon arch per year is enough for me."

Rachel laughed, delighted that the last pieces of the gala were coming together. The children's choir would sound amazing, and Scott had turned a hotel in the tiny town of Sunset Cove into a must-see fundraising destination. Rachel wrapped her arms around her waist, squeezing herself as she continued to look around the room. "It's incredible. I'm so glad you asked me to be part of this. My students will be thrilled. We've never performed anywhere this special."

"That's the point, remember? The hospital expansion will benefit kids, so they should play a role in making it happen." He held up a hand and gestured for her to wait. "Give me a minute. I've got one more surprise."

Scott walked behind the risers and fiddled with a small speaker system. He pulled out his phone and tapped a few buttons, causing slow music to play as he set down his phone and walked back to Rachel's side.

He held out his arms, wrapping one around her back and clasping her hand in the other, leaving enough space for her sling between them. "We haven't checked out the dance floor or acoustics yet," he explained. "It's an important part of the process."

Rachel smiled and let herself snuggle closer as they swayed to the music. "Very important," she agreed. "You don't want the gala guests to be disappointed."

Scott looked down into her eyes, amusement playing across his face. "I'm not worried about the gala right now. I just wanted an excuse to dance with you."

Rachel thought she might float away as they gently swayed to the music. Neither of them had strong dancing skills, but that was okay. Like Scott said, what mattered was that they were close to each other. Rachel put her head on his chest, noting that their height difference was an advantage at times like this.

Is this what love is like? she wondered. *Slow dances, and two hearts beating as one. Knowing that the person in your arms would do anything to protect you—and you would do the same in return.* The encounter with Cory had scared her, but she knew that between Scott and herself, they could handle almost anything.

This might be love, she realized, holding back a laugh. It was funny how life snuck up on you, handing you the right person when you least expected it.

Rachel lifted her head higher, letting herself enjoy the smell of his cologne and clean skin. It had been a long time since she'd been close to a man. It had been even longer since she'd let a man be so close to her heart.

The song ended. Scott held her for a moment longer, then sighed as an ad for a car dealership blasted over the speaker system. "Thank you for the dance. We might be too busy to dance tomorrow night. I'm glad I got at least one song with you."

Rachel looked up and smiled. "Save the last dance for me, too."

"It's a deal."

Twenty-four hours later, she found herself back in her tiny apartment, adjusting the sling around her neck with quick, sharp movements.

"I can't wait to get this thing off," she said, trying to protect her arm as she fussed with the slim black dress she'd chosen for the gala. Her cast was finally off, but her arm was still tender. The doctor had recommended the sling for a week or two—and as much as she hated the hindrance, it helped with the discomfort.

Brook stood beside Rachel and steadied her hands. "It's for the best. You'll hurt yourself if you do things too soon. Besides, it matches your dress. Wasn't it nice of Scott to find you a new sling?"

Rachel grunted as she examined the silky black contraption. It was a lot better than the dark blue sling she'd used to hold her heavy cast, and at least the cast was gone. Rachel reminded herself to be optimistic. Her kids were ready, and she'd been leading them through their songs with one arm for weeks. Everything would be fine.

It had been a good idea to invite her friends over. Rachel had picked out this dress ages ago, back when she had two working arms. The zipper running down her back had been a problem. She'd nearly needed to ask a neighbor to zip her up. How mortifying.

Emma rushed to her side with a hairbrush and curling iron. She smiled as she brushed out Rachel's hair. "Thanks for letting us help you. My kid says she's too old to let me do her hair now." Emma rolled her eyes and frowned. "Kendra's only eight. She made alternative plans when she heard about tonight. What's she gonna be like when she's a teenager?"

"She'll be a perfectly behaved young lady, just like her mother." Brook grinned and grabbed the plug to the curling iron, walking it to the nearby outlet. "When she doesn't act like a sweet young woman, you're welcome to stop by the bakery and drown your sorrow in cupcakes and coffee."

Rachel chuckled. Aside from working at the bakery, she wasn't spending enough time with her friends. The small talk and support did her heart good. Most of her friends didn't have family nearby. Instead, they'd cobbled together a family of their own.

She fanned away a few tears as Emma began curling her hair. "Thanks again. For everything. I don't know what I'd do without you."

Emma smiled back. "You would do the same for us. Besides, you broke your arm protecting a student. I'm not a teacher, but I am a mom. And I'm so grateful the kids on that bus made it home."

"And you're raising a ton of money for the children's center," Brook pointed out. "You can drive by that hospital and be proud. You helped build something important for this town."

Rachel's lip trembled. "Why did you say that? You're making me cry." Her hand moved at a faster tempo, fanning the tears that formed. "I don't have time to redo my makeup!"

Laughter filled the apartment as they all burst into giggles. Rachel shook her head. What a crazy way to start the gala. She was glad Brook and Emma had come over.

Finding time to date was hard enough. Juggling schedules with friends was just as difficult, but even more important.

Chapter Twenty-Six

Scott

SCOTT TUGGED AT THE bow tie he'd worn to the gala. At least stethoscopes had a useful function. He felt silly in his suit and tie, but it was important to look the part.

Tonight, he wasn't just Scott. He was Dr. Scott Hart, Director of Pediatric Medicine at Sunset Cove Community Hospital.

The title had a nice ring to it. More importantly, he was moving away from the crazy hours and relentless workload. Soon he wouldn't need to tackle the dual jobs of emergency room physician and director of the center's expansion.

He'd spoken to Dr. Sonya Epstein this morning, and she would replace him as head of the pediatric emergency room in a few weeks. Things were finally coming together.

Once Sonya settled into his old job, Scott could focus on Rachel. Build a more normal life, with a schedule closer to the rest of the world.

Until then, it would be chaos as usual. He would make it work. Carve out time for Rachel, and show she was still important to him—even when they weren't working together.

Any thoughts of romance would need to wait a few more hours, though. His marketing department had done a phenomenal job with today's fundraiser. They'd sold out of tickets and brought dozens of new sponsors into the hospital's growing network.

Tonight was going to be great, but they were also setting a foundation for something even bigger.

Rachel had made their job easier. People noticed her in the community, organizing a choir featuring their children and grandchildren. Hosting fun runs and basket raffles. Every minute of exposure she'd given the hospital was worth hours of direct contact with sponsors, begging them for money.

Scott's heart warmed as he thought about the woman waiting with her students. Some giggles came from the room behind the choir's risers, but Rachel was keeping the kids in line. They'd start in a few minutes.

Scott hoped the kids were excited. They had worked hard for this moment, and those kids deserved to shine.

He checked his pocket. Scott had set aside a surprise for Rachel. She deserved a moment in the spotlight, too.

"You've done a great job tonight." William, the hospital's CEO, came behind Scott to pat him on the back. His wife and an older couple stood with him. "I was telling my friends from upstate about the work you've put into the silent auction. Mr. and Mrs. Hunt, this is Dr. Scott Hart. He's the man I've told you about."

Scott smiled and resisted the urge to tug at his tie again. "It's a pleasure to meet you," he replied, trying to guess which part of the auction would most appeal to William's friends. "Have you looked through the bidding table? There's a week-long house rental in Paris."

"I've always wanted to visit France," Mrs. Hunt exclaimed. "We've never been overseas. It sounds like a wonderful adventure. Very romantic." She turned to her husband, who smiled back indulgently.

"Now's your chance. There are also some excellent vacation opportunities closer to home." Scott had always excelled at reading people. It was an ability he'd developed in the emergency room.

Would your patient be angry and defiant, or helpful and honest? It was nice to use his talents for a larger purpose, like raising money for the center. "Don't forget, every dollar supports our new children's division."

"I've heard you've raised a lot of money," Mr. Hunt said. "You've left quite a mark already. You're a regular hometown hero, I'd say."

Scott shook his head. "I'm no hero. These kids deserve the best we can give them. I'm just doing my job and making sure that happens. The real heroes are the doctors we're hiring for the new pediatric ward. They'll change children's lives."

"Don't be modest," William added. "You've changed thousands of lives."

Scott shrugged off the compliment and urged the Hunts toward the bidding table.

Was he a hero? He'd never given it much thought. To Scott, real heroes were the surgeons who operated on tiny babies. Nurses who restarted a child's heart after cardiac arrest. Teachers who shielded their students from harm, even if it meant risking their own injuries.

Heroes were pretty brunettes with bright purple casts.

Scott shook off that thought and continued to move through the crowd, welcoming people and thanking them for their support. He wanted every person to leave happy, well-fed, and ready to spread the word about their pediatric ward. They'd need ongoing donations to get the expansion built and staffed.

But while tonight's work was important, Scott would rather be behind the scenes—with Rachel, instead of shaking hands with people in the ballroom.

He'd give any excuse for another dance.

Scott thought back to William's friends. Mr. Hunt had looked proud and content, happy to hold his wife's hand and encourage her dreams about visiting Paris.

Maybe Rachel would like Paris, he thought. *I should place a bid, too.*

Scott chuckled and shook his head. His new title and promotion came with a healthy salary, but he hoped tonight's bidding went far beyond his budget. Their fundraiser depended on it.

Besides, he still owed Rachel a dolphin-watching trip. They didn't need to leave town to have fun together.

Scott's phone vibrated in his pocket, interrupting his thoughts. He frowned as the hospital's number flashed across his screen. They had security on site tonight. A message from them was a bad sign.

His fingers flew across the screen as he logged into the hospital's messaging app.

SCCH Security

> Man without ticket at the front door. Says he's with the choir.

Scott groaned. This wasn't something he could handle alone. He'd need to pull Rachel from the choir and hope they had enough chaperones to watch the students. She could identify the parent, or speak with the child, and decide if they should be allowed backstage.

He read over the message again. Something about the situation made him uncomfortable. A parent at the school was targeting Rachel, and most of the children had arrived with their parents.

> I'll meet you at the front entrance.

Scott put his phone away and worked his way through the crowd. His eyes hardened when he spotted Cory Wilde standing next to the security guard. He was grateful he'd left Rachel with her students. She was safer with the other parents and children.

"You're not welcome here," Scott said quietly. "Please leave now, before I have to call the police."

Cory didn't bother keeping his voice down. "You can't stop me. The other parents are backstage," he bellowed, causing a couple on the red carpet to startle and walk more quickly toward the ballroom.

Scott's vision flashed red as anger surged through this body. "Sir, I can and will stop you. We allow custodial parents and guardians backstage. You do not have custody of your daughter."

Scott considered mentioning the restraining order that his ex-wife and Rachel had filed against him, but thought better of it. No need to fan the flames. "You should leave. If you would like to watch your daughter perform, our PR team will post a video tomorrow."

He hadn't expected his words to calm down Mr. Wilde. What Scott didn't predict was that the man would lunge toward him and grab his jacket. Scott froze in surprise.

"I don't know who you are, but you're not keeping me from my daughter," Cory hissed. "That teacher can't keep me from my daughter, either. You both need to be taught a lesson."

Scott braced himself and protected his face with his arm, refusing to throw the first punch. He prayed that this wouldn't turn into a fight. *Not tonight. Not in front of everyone who's supported our children's center.*

Onlookers gasped as the security guard pulled Cory off Scott and wrestled his arms behind his back.

Scott had never been more relieved to let security do their job. He heard handcuffs click into place, causing the dad to howl in outrage. Tonight's battle was over—and this might be the last of Cory Wilde. Once the dad was in police custody, he'd be in plenty of trouble. Cory was violating a restraining order, for starters. He was also trespassing at a private event.

Thank you, God, he thought. Scott took a shaky breath and watched the security guard radio for backup, pulling Cory into a corner and away from the main entrance.

This was not part of tonight's plan. But Rachel was still safe, and Scott would do anything to keep her that way. She'd find out about Mr. Wilde's presence later—but not right now. Not when it was time for her to go on stage.

Scott took another deep breath and followed the security guard. "Do you need anything else?"

The guard shook his head. "The police are on their way. I've got hotel backup, too." He gestured toward the door as two more security guards strode toward them.

Scott glanced at the clock and nodded. The entire situation had taken less than five minutes. "Good job tonight. Thanks for stopping him."

He steadied his nerves and tugged at his suit, straightening the coat and fixing the tie that had gone sideways.

Time to support his favorite woman and children's choir.

Chapter Twenty-Seven

Rachel

RACHEL PULLED BACK THE heavy door separating the choir's waiting area from the ballroom, trying to peek out at the gala's guests. People in tuxedos and fancy dresses filled the room.

Her eyes widened at the size of the crowd. Scott had said they'd sold every ticket. She'd believed him, but Rachel hadn't realized how many tickets were available for sale.

She smiled as a dozen couples gathered in the center of the room, all dancing to the string quartet's music. It reminded her of last night's dance with Scott. She'd grown closer to Scott than she thought possible—and they weren't even dating yet. Not officially.

"Ms. Lancaster, you said no peeking," Emily reminded her in a whisper. "If you can see the audience, they can see you! We don't wanna ruin the mood."

Rachel smiled down at Emily. She'd assembled the sweetest group of children. They weren't professional singers, but she hoped the crowd would be pleased. These were real kids from Sunset Cove, and the children that the hospital hoped to help.

They might not sing every note on key, but these kids had heart. And wasn't tonight all about the children?

Rachel snuck one last look out at the crowd. If only she could glimpse Scott before she gathered the choir's attention...

There he was! Her heart beat faster as he walked into the ballroom, looking more handsome than ever.

It had been hard enough finding time to meet when they worked together. Could they mean something to each other, and mesh their crazy schedules, without a project binding them? She hoped they could.

Enough thinking about Scott. It's time to focus now, she scolded herself. *Let's blow this crowd away with our performance.*

"Everyone, it's almost time!" she called. "We're on stage in five minutes. Line up in order!"

Rachel grabbed her list of students and helped them shuffle into place. The shortest ones would stand in the front; now they just needed to stay in one spot for a few minutes, and walk onto the risers like they'd practiced.

She smiled at the children, attempting to make eye contact with every boy and girl in line. "I could not be more pleased with this group. You've worked so hard to make this happen. We've overcome challenges." She gestured to her arm and sling, making a few of the parents chuckle. "We learned to work together. You've stood up for yourselves and your choir members. You committed to this project, and you stuck to that commitment. I am so proud of everything you've done this year."

Rachel took a deep breath and promised herself that she wouldn't cry. Now wasn't the time for tears. She could cry afterward, when she celebrated how well they'd done. She reminded the choir that they should wait for Scott's introduction, then cracked the door open to listen for his voice.

Scott began speaking as the string quartet ended its song. "May I have your attention, please?" He paused for a moment, giving the crowd time to turn toward him and stop talking. "Thank you all for supporting the Sunset Cove Community Hospital. I hope you're enjoying yourself tonight."

Rachel grinned as he paused again, this time waiting for the applause to end.

"I've got a real treat for you tonight. I'm about to bring out Sunset Cove Elementary School's children's choir." Scott glanced toward the door. "They've been practicing since Easter, preparing these songs just for you. None of this would be possible without their amazing choir director, Ms. Rachel Lancaster. Ms. Lancaster, can you come out here?"

Rachel's eyes widened as she jumped back from the door. What was he doing? They hadn't talked about a personal introduction. He was supposed to introduce the choir. She would walk out with her students.

"Ms. Lancaster, he said your name!" one of her students hissed. "Should we come with you, or are you going by yourself first?"

She looked at her students and raised her chin. "We started this together. Let's finish this together, too."

Rachel smiled as her students filed out of the room, walking to the bleachers while the crowd clapped. Scott waited until every child was in place, then looked down at Rachel, beaming with pride.

"I met Ms. Lancaster by chance a few months ago. When I learned she was a music teacher, it gave me an idea for tonight's fundraiser. What if we could bring together a children's choir? Give the town's kids a chance to show us their talent, and demonstrate why a pediatric unit is needed in Sunset County."

Scott turned to the children on the risers. "Somewhere along the way, this grew into something bigger. Your school raised thousands of dollars in its own fundraiser. That's all thanks to Ms. Lancaster. You've also told your parents to support the hospital. A few parents went to their employers, and they made donations. We can trace a *half-million dollars* back to the children of Sunset Elementary. What do you think about that?"

Rachel gasped, staring at Scott as her students cheered. She knew the school had asked parents to consider donating, and they'd raised a good amount with the basket raffle and run. The final tally still blew her away.

Scott reached out and steadied her, smiling down at Rachel before he turned back to address the crowd. "We'll be putting that money to good use. The money that the school, and all of you here, have raised will allow us to staff and expand our pediatric unit faster than we ever thought possible. To thank all of you, we're installing a permanent version of today's 'walk of fame' in our new emergency room waiting area. I'm happy to announce that Sunset Cove Elementary School will have one of those stars."

He reached into his pocket and pulled out a small gold star, holding it up for the crowd. "This is a smaller version of the stars we'll use at the hospital. Rachel, can you please tell us what it says?"

Rachel held out a trembling hand to accept the star. She swallowed the lump in her throat, then read the engraved words while Scott held a microphone for her. "'To Rachel Lancaster and the children of Sunset Cove Elementary School: Thank you for showing us the heart of Sunset Cove.'" She took a breath and let it out slowly, tears falling from her eyes. "Thank you, Scott. And thank you to everyone who donated tonight. I can't wait to see our stars in the new emergency room."

"But no rush," Scott added, turning back to the students with a mock sternness. "There's no rush to visit our new unit! I want every child here to stay healthy and uninjured."

The crowd laughed, giving Rachel a chance to chuckle and compose herself. Scott patted her on the back and gestured toward the choir. It was time to perform.

Rachel wiped away a stray tear and stepped in front of her choir. She turned on the tablet in front of her, making sure her music was on the right page. Then she raised her good arm, and the children began to sing.

Scott may have joked about testing the acoustics of the hall, but Rachel's choir had never performed in a space so grand ... or so large. Their eyes brightened with delight as they heard their voices mingle in the air, mixing in a beautiful harmony.

The audience was silent, their attention pulled toward the choir as they sang "This is Me." These weren't professional showmen. Still, their innocence and sweet voices added a depth that made Rachel fight back more tears. These kids should be proud of what they had become. They had worked together to make their town a better place. Even the biggest bullies in the school couldn't take that away.

When they were done, Aubrey stepped forward from her spot on the risers. "Thank you for coming today! My name is Aubrey O'Grady, and I am eleven years old. I am also a cancer survivor."

The audience turned silent, focusing its joint attention on the young girl.

She stood tall, not seeming to mind the hundreds of eyes turned toward her. "Eighteen months ago, I was diagnosed with lymphoma, a type of blood cancer. It was really scary, and really hard. But the hardest part of my diagnosis was traveling to CHOP so often. I missed school and couldn't see my friends. My parents took a lot of time off work."

Aubrey smiled out at the crowd, where Rachel knew her parents were watching.

"Once our pediatric hospital is open, kids like me won't have to travel so far for care. It's one less thing they'll have to worry about. And that makes me happy. I've been in remission for six months, and I hope Dr. Hart can help lots of other kids get to remission, too." She paused again and gave Scott a thumbs up. "Thank you for coming tonight, and for letting us sing! Our next song is 'I Lived' by One Republic, featuring soloist Emily Wilde."

Rachel's heart nearly burst with pride as Aubrey climbed back onto the risers. *It must take so much strength to talk about her journey*, she thought. *These kids are amazing.*

Emily stepped into place at the front of the choir, and Rachel pressed the "play" button on her music player. Emily's sweet voice filled the hall, singing a song about taking chances and living life to its fullest.

It was a beautiful way to end the performance.

Chapter Twenty-Eight

Scott

Scott looked around the ballroom with pride.

He'd talked to Rachel and Mrs. Wilde privately, letting them know about Cory's attempts to enter the party. Both women were happy to hand matters over to the police.

But despite the disruption Cory Wilde had caused, it had been a wonderful night. The CEO had announced the top bidders of the silent auction an hour before. Between tonight's gala and the school fundraiser, the hospital would receive almost two million dollars—more than enough to open the first stage of the children's ward.

While Mr. and Mrs. Hunt hadn't won a trip to Paris in the auction, they had won a two-week stay at Sunset Cove's best bed-and-breakfast. Mrs. Hunt would return in the fall, when the weather was cooler and the town's fall festivals were in full swing. They would have a great time.

Scott was looking forward to the fall festivals, too. He'd heard the lighthouse festival was worth visiting. If he was lucky, he'd have a more flexible schedule by fall—and a special woman to keep him company as they climbed toward the best views in Sunset Cove.

Scott smiled as Rachel walked toward him. They'd had a long night, but it wasn't over yet. A few guests still lingered. He needed to mingle and nudge them out the door.

Then Scott could head back to his apartment for a few hours of sleep. His next shift started tomorrow morning at seven.

But he didn't tell Rachel any of that. Instead, he continued to smile and held out a hand. If he'd learned anything these last few months, it was to prioritize the important people in his life. Let the trustees mingle. No one would miss Scott if he wandered off for a few minutes.

They each grabbed a bottle of water and took one last walk through the ballroom. She marveled at the walk of fame, where Scott had added a star for the elementary school. The hospital's maintenance team would move the cling stickers to their front foyer tomorrow, where they would stay until permanent stars could replace them.

"Such a lovely surprise," she murmured. "I can't believe the school raised so much money."

Scott shook his head, tipping Rachel's chin up to look her in the eyes. "It wasn't the school. It was you. From the day we met to discuss the fundraiser, you've encouraged everyone you know to help."

"I tried to quit," she admitted. "When I saw where we'd perform, I thought the kids wouldn't be good enough. They proved me wrong. I'm glad we stuck with it."

They continued out the door into a courtyard lit with fairy lights. Scott tugged her toward a small gazebo and swing. They sat down, swinging gently in the cool night air.

"What kept you from quitting?"

Rachel let the swing's movement move her back and forth, deep in thought. "My friends talked me out of it. Thinking about Aubrey helped. We watched her go through so much during cancer treatment. I also couldn't let down Emily, or Jude, or any of the kids who made tonight happen. If they could be strong enough to get through this, I could be too."

Scott smiled and shook his head. He turned toward Rachel, taking her hand in his. "I'm glad your students give you strength. But have you looked in the mirror lately?" He paused as she tilted her head in confusion. "You were strong enough to face your fears. That's why you didn't quit. You didn't just push through a tough project. You inspired an entire community. Rachel, you inspired me, too."

Rachel blushed and stared at their joined hands. "Where do we go from here?"

He laughed and reached up to brush a strand of hair off her face. "I jump back into my crazy schedule tomorrow morning. You've got the summer off from school, but you're working at the bakery. I hope you'll still find time for me, though."

"I'd like that," she admitted quietly. "Things will be different, though. We're not working together anymore."

"And we're not juggling a fundraiser on top of our busy schedules. This could be a good thing."

They leaned back in the swing, content to watch the stars shine as they listened to the string quartet entertain the last guests. The music would stop soon enough. Their lives would go back to normal. Scott knew he should ask Rachel for one last dance, but he was content just to sit by her side.

Is this what love feels like? he wondered. *Stealing quiet moments together, content to enjoy the other person's company?*

He wasn't sure what this was, but he liked it.

When the music stopped, Scott stood and reached for Rachel's hand. "We should go. I need to say 'goodbye' to guests. And I'm sure you're working early in the bakery tomorrow."

Rachel sighed and nodded. "Hungry customers won't wait. When will I see you again?"

Scott looked up at the stars, twinkling like diamonds in the sky. He couldn't believe how *beautiful* everything was in Sunset Cove.

The sky, the ocean, and the woman sitting next to him. "We still need to plan our boat ride. I'll text you about that. And I'll try to see you at the bakery."

"It's a date," she said brightly, then blushed at her use of words. "Unless it's not a date. It doesn't need to be."

Scott squeezed her hand and held tight. "If you don't know that answer by now, I haven't been clear enough." He looked down at her, his face lit up with a smile. "You're an amazing woman, and I'd be a fool to let you walk away. Let's go on a date. Lots of dates. It will take some work to get our schedules coordinated, but you're worth the effort."

Scott held his breath as he searched Rachel's face, looking for some sort of response. To his relief, her lips tugged upward in a smile.

"It's a date, Dr. Hart. I'll wait for your phone call. Have a nice night."

Scott raised her hand to his lips and left a single kiss on her knuckles. They walked inside, dropping hands only when she reached the room leading to the choir's staging area. Then they parted ways—Rachel checking for her students' forgotten belongings, and Scott guiding the last of the guests out the door.

When he was done, the choir's room was empty. Rachel was gone. But she'd left behind the scent of her floral perfume, and the promise of more magical days ahead.

Chapter Twenty-Nine

Rachel

RACHEL SLAMMED THE OVEN door shut, rattling its metal frame. She pivoted to the cooling racks and slid a piping-hot tray of chocolate muffins into the stand.

She spun around to put cookies into the empty oven—and nearly plowed into Brook.

Brook held up her hands in defense. "Easy there. Don't take your anger out on my kitchen. If you need to vent, I'd recommend making bread." She pointed to the counter at a mound of dough. "Punching dough is very cathartic. Breaking my oven doors, not so much."

Rachel snorted and slid the cookies into the oven, then gently closed the door. "I'll knead the bread, but I'm not angry. And I don't need to vent."

Brook sat on one of the kitchen's bar stools and tipped her chair back with a laugh. "That's the funniest thing I've heard today. You've been slamming around this kitchen since five o'clock. Something's got you worked up. What's wrong?"

Rachel punched and pounded the bread dough, trying to gather her thoughts. Brook was right—making bread felt better than slamming oven doors. Rachel was happy to use both arms again, too. She'd started leaving the sling at home a few days ago. Her arm had finally healed.

Rachel continued to fold and punch the dough until her friend cleared her throat.

"I can wait all day." Brook glanced at the clock. "Actually, I have ten minutes until Avery's shift is over. Then one of us has to run the register. But tell me what's wrong. I'm a good listener."

To her horror, a tear drifted down Rachel's cheek. She caught it with her shirt sleeve, wiping the tear away before it fell into the dough. No need to spoil the bread with salt water and germs.

Rachel sighed and pushed the dough away, then washed her hands and grabbed the chair next to Brook. "It's been two weeks since the gala, and I haven't heard from Scott. I thought he'd call by now." She stared at the ceiling, willing her eyes to stay dry. "Adam texted me last night. He invited me to the hospital's end-of-summer picnic. He probably thought he was doing me a favor. But I wanted to hear from Scott, not Adam."

"Of course you did." Brook cocked her head to the side. "Did you try texting Scott? Did he reply, or is he ghosting you?"

Rachel shook her head. "No, I haven't texted him." She flinched as Brook raised her eyebrows. "I know. Communication goes both ways. But I wanted him to reach out first. Put a little effort into calling me."

Brook shook her head as she stood and walked over to the counter. She greased the bread pans, pausing to look over her shoulder at her friend. "You're playing a dangerous game. Sometimes you've got to make the first move. We're adults now. We can't sit at home, waiting for a call."

Rachel nodded and scrunched up her face. "You're right. I'm being ridiculous. I'll text him after my shift."

"Do it now," Brook urged her. "While you have time and you're thinking about him."

Am I ever not *thinking about him?* she wondered, glancing at her phone on the desk. Scott filled her thoughts all day long. She'd like to think she was on his mind, too. But if that was the case, he should have called by now.

Besides, he'd promised to text last week. They were still supposed to go on the dolphin-watching boat together. Maybe he'd forgotten.

Unless he'd changed his mind.

Stop it, she chastised herself. *He didn't change his mind. He'd just too busy to make time for you.*

It shocked Rachel to realize how hurt she felt. Her students were her top priority, and Scott's work at the hospital always came first. As it should. But they'd never make a relationship work if they couldn't find time for each other.

He just hasn't had time yet, she told herself.

But if they waited much longer, it would be too late. School would start soon. Her days would be filled with children and music. Tourist season would be over, too. The tour boats worked for a few weeks into the fall, but they packed away their vessels before winter. Rachel had watched them pull the boats out of the harbor and into dry storage at the start of last year's hurricane season.

Late summer and autumn were her favorite seasons. This year, not so much. Her chance with Scott was slipping away with each passing day.

Still, she didn't want to seem desperate. Rachel wouldn't scare him away by texting or calling every day. So instead, she sat alone. Waiting for him to call.

"Earth to Rachel," Brook said, snapping her fingers. She slid Rachel's phone across the counter. "Text him now," she repeated.

Rachel turned on her phone and twisted her lips as she checked the time. "Can't do it, boss. Avery's leaving in two minutes. I've got to clean up and deal with the cash register."

Brook threw up her hands. "Fine. Don't complain to me when I'm married with five kids, and you're still wondering, 'Why hasn't Scott called me yet?'"

Rachel burst out laughing as she took off her apron and tossed it into the laundry pile. "Five kids. You're not even married to Brad yet. Is there something you're not telling me?"

Brook joined in her friend's laughter and shook her head. "Of course not. We're still trying to pick a wedding date. It can't be during tourist season, and Brad's schedule won't slow down this year. The hospital expansion will keep them busy all winter. It'll keep Scott busy, too. Keep that in mind."

Rachel stopped laughing and looked up in surprise. "I thought the expansion would be done by the start of the school year."

"The first stage, yes. I'm sure Scott's working frantically right now, trying to hire enough staff to run their emergency room before it opens." Brook added a dusting of flour to her bread dough, then covered the pans to rise one last time. "The construction crew's moving to the second floor soon. Remember all those doctors' offices? Scott's life can't be easy now. Give him a break—text him first. Say that you miss him. Don't let work come between you."

Rachel considered her friend's words as she checked her image in the kitchen mirror, wiping some stray flour off her face. She added a clean apron and tied it behind her back.

Brook was right. Scott had been clear enough about his intentions. They knew they'd have to work hard to find time together, especially now that they didn't schedule "dates" around a joint project.

He'd promised to text her. But when he hadn't, Rachel should have reached out. Checked to see if he was okay. Instead, she had hidden in her quiet apartment and cried. Rachel hung her head.

She was a better friend, and a better person. She grabbed her phone and opened the texting app just as the kitchen door flew open.

Avery rushed inside, pulling off her own apron to reveal a growing baby bump. "Got to go. Sophia's swim practice ends in thirty minutes, and I promised I'd watch the end. All okay?"

Brook smiled as her friend tossed the apron through the air. "No problem. You told me about swim practice last week. We can handle things."

Avery nodded, blew a kiss, and rushed out the door and into her car.

Brook gestured toward Avery's car as it pulled into traffic. "That's how you make family a priority. Tell me what you need, and we'll make it happen." She smiled and added the dirty apron to the laundry pile. "We're three busy women with a growing business. Family still comes first."

"Scott isn't family."

"Not yet." Brook walked to the kitchen door and held it open, gesturing for Rachel to take over the front of the shop. "Work with the customers. You'll have more time to text Scott."

Rachel felt lighter as she walked into the customers' side of Seaside Cupcakes. Maybe all she needed was a little more communication with Scott. In any case, it was time to find out. She pulled her phone out of her pocket and opened the texting app again—only to be interrupted by the bell ringing over the shop door.

She chuckled darkly. Communication was important, but it wouldn't happen during her shift, would it? Rachel slid the phone back into her pocket.

Most of the summer customers were tourists. To her surprise, she knew this customer. Adam walked through the door with a big grin.

"Good, you're here," he said. "I hoped you were working today. Why didn't you reply to my text?"

Rachel bit her lip and tried to come up with an excuse. She couldn't admit that his message had made her cry. She'd even silenced her phone for the night. "I was too tired, and then I forgot. Sorry about that," she said with false cheerfulness. "Who's coming to the picnic?"

"Scott will be there." Adam wiggled his eyebrows. "I know you haven't seen him in two weeks. The man's gotten grumpier every day without you. Just call him or stop by. He doesn't get regular lunch breaks in the emergency room, but he'll find a few minutes for you."

Rachel frowned as all of her insecurities came flooding back. It was like Brook's pep talk had never happened. "Are you sure he wants to see me?"

Adam nodded and frowned. "He's been trying to text you. Reception is spotty inside the hospital, and there's no time to step outside." He ran a hand through his hair and sighed. "We're swamped with tourists right now. Kids playing with jellyfish. Drunk people with sprained ankles. Being tipsy on heels isn't cute, by the way."

She nodded and agreed. Alcohol and tourists didn't mix. "He's busy. I don't want to bother him."

"He's also interviewing staff members every day of the week." Adam continued, as if Rachel hadn't spoken. "Nurses, emergency room physicians, even Child Life candidates and social workers. He wants the new unit to run perfectly, so he's made a point of sitting in on every interview."

Adam paused and pointed to the display case. "Give me two dozen cookies, please. Add some brownies or cupcakes. Mix it up. The hospital staff needs a treat after this week."

Rachel grabbed a box and filled it with chocolate chip cookies, a few brownies, and a half-dozen strawberry cupcakes with whipped frosting. She glanced back at the kitchen door, knowing that Brook wouldn't mind her generosity. "It's on the house. Thanks for working so hard to keep our town healthy."

"Thanks. We appreciate that." He pulled a twenty-dollar bill out of his wallet and stuffed it into the tip jar. "Now, what about the hospital picnic? I need to RSVP this week. It's between shift changes, so everyone gets to attend before or after work."

Rachel hesitated. It would be an excuse to see Scott, especially if they couldn't connect soon. Hopefully, she wouldn't seem too eager if she showed up at a company picnic. "Are you sure I'm invited? I don't work at the hospital."

"It's fine." Adam waved off her concern. "You raised a lot of money for us. We'd love to make you an honorary employee. Besides, Scott's allowed to bring a plus-one. I can RSVP for the two of you together—or bring you as my guest, if that makes you more comfortable."

Rachel flinched, thinking about how embarrassed she would be as Adam's guest. He was a nice-enough guy—but he was also Scott's friend. She didn't want to give Scott the wrong impression. "Make me an honorary employee, please." She slid the bakery box into a bag and handed it across the counter. "Thanks for the invitation. It sounds like fun."

Adam took the box and bobbed his head in farewell. But he hesitated as he headed toward the door. "He's doing this for you."

"Doing what?" Rachel's eyebrows knitted in confusion.

"Meeting with the construction crew on his days off. Working overtime to staff our unit and find his own replacement. Once the pediatric unit opens, he'll be the new director. He won't work in the emergency room anymore."

"Oh." Rachel let out a soft breath as she considered Adam's words. "He's quitting his job?"

Adam shook his head. "He was never supposed to do it all. Scott's doing the work of two men right now. Once his replacement starts, he'll have a better schedule. He's working overtime now, to free up time in the future. For you." He smiled and put a hand on the door. "Have a great day. I'll see you at the picnic."

Rachel stared out the door, watching Adam climb into his car and drive away. Was Scott really working so hard for her? No one had done that for her before.

She tugged her phone out of its pocket and typed out a message.

Chapter Thirty

Scott

SCOTT WAS SO BUSY that he wanted to scream.

Unfortunately, that would be counterproductive. If he started yelling from his desk near the head nurse, staff would come running. That would cause an even bigger backlog. Dozens of adults and children were waiting to be seen.

Scott had seen busy emergency rooms, but nothing like this. Tourist season at the shore was no joke.

He'd been trying to text Rachel for days. He had a list of dates for the dolphin-watching tour. The boat owner only ran sunrise tours twice a week, so their choices were limited. But every time he picked up his phone, Scott got pulled away.

The two times he slipped away to text Rachel, the message had bounced back. No service. Try again later.

When he *did* have time and cell phone service, exhaustion took over. It took all Scott's energy to shower off the hospital germs before falling into bed.

Things would get better, he reminded himself. Sonya was replacing him in three weeks. Still, Sonya wouldn't be here until the start of the school year. Rachel's busy season would start just as his was ending.

Scott sighed and pulled out his phone. Such lousy excuses. If he was going to find time for Rachel, he needed to do it now. Not three weeks from now. A tour boat had been available that morning. He couldn't switch his hospital shifts, but it was another reminder that they needed to pick a date soon.

> Hey! Not avoiding you. Want to go on a boat ride Thursday?

Scott stared at the screen without sending the message. Was it too flippant? What if Rachel had changed her mind? He deleted the words and started again.

> Hi! I miss spending time with you.

Better. Or maybe worse. He sounded desperate, even if it was true.

> There are boat rides this Thursday. Are you available?

Much better. His finger hovered over the "send" button, hesitating only for a moment before he committed.

System error
> Signal unavailable. Message not sent.

Scott groaned and tossed his phone on the desk in frustration, then picked it up again. He'd need to walk out to the parking lot to get decent cell service. He would take a minute to do that now.

Scott stood up and strode toward the exit just as his phone pinged.

> **Pediatric head trauma. ETA 3 minutes.**

Scott sighed and closed his eyes, centering himself on the task at hand. Patients came first. They always came first. He hoped Rachel would understand and forgive his silence.

·♥·♥·♥·♥·♥·

Once his patient was stabilized and headed out for a CT scan, Scott headed back to his desk. The kid had hit his head on the bottom of a swimming pool and knocked himself unconscious. Fortunately, dad had pulled him out of the water right away.

His patient would be fine. They'd do testing and observe him overnight to be sure. If they were lucky, the kid wouldn't need to transfer to a larger children's hospital.

I still need to text Rachel, he thought, pivoting from his desk toward the staff exit.

This time, one of his nurses stopped Scott.

"I've got a mom eager for discharge. Can you sign her son's paperwork?" Amy Ross, his newest hire, held out her laptop with a tired smile. "We've got quite a line in the waiting room."

"Never look at the waiting room queue," he advised her, scanning the document in front of him before scribbling his signature on the discharge form. "Triage will push the sickest patients to the front. Our job is to focus on the kids in our rooms."

She nodded and took the tablet, heading back to her patient's room. Then Amy turned with a bright smile and called, "Adam's shift ended an hour ago, but he's bringing back donuts. They'll be in the break room."

He got those donuts from Rachel, Scott realized. Lucky guy. Not for the first time, he envied his nurses' ability to work eight-hour shifts. It made getting out into the real world easier.

Scott glanced at his computer screen and sorted his patients by priority, then headed into the next child's exam room. He needed to take his own advice and focus on the kids in front of him. There wouldn't be time to visit the parking lot today.

He rounded on three patients before Adam rushed into the unit.

"I've got cupcakes! Brownies! Cookies! Freshly made with love." Adam walked two steps behind Scott, letting the scent of baked goods follow him down the hallway.

"I've got one more patient to check on, and a CT scan to review. Save me a cupcake?" Scott didn't break stride as he headed into the next exam room.

When he returned to his desk, Adam was waiting with a cupcake and two cookies. "Thought you could use a pick-me-up," he explained. "Did you eat anything today?"

Scott's stomach grumbled in response. "I had breakfast. That was only... seven hours ago. I didn't get to the cafeteria."

Adam shook his head and held out the plate. "Have some food. Then take a walk. You need a break."

"I didn't review the CT scan yet," Scott said, shoving a cookie into his mouth. He chewed quickly and took a sip of water to wash it down, startled to realize his water bottle was still full. Had he gone seven hours without drinking? Scott was a doctor. He should know better.

"Did radiology message you?" Adam asked.

"No. But my patient's back in his room."

"If radiology didn't flag the scan, there's no emergency. Read the report, follow up with the patient, and then take a walk." Adam looked up at his friend and frowned. "Go to the cafeteria. Or walk to your car and back. Do something outside these four walls."

"I don't have time for a walk. I've got to prep for another staff interview. We might fill our last spot today."

Adam shook his head. "You need to get out of emergency medicine. I'll miss working with you, but it's time to move to the pediatric unit full-time. No more working two jobs at once."

Scott frowned, realizing that his friend was right. They didn't talk about mental health and self-care in medical school, but he'd seen enough doctors burn out. "Okay, I'm taking a break. Right after I read this scan and update the patient's family."

Adam crossed his arms and stood at the desk. "I'm not leaving until you're done, just to make sure it happens. You'll be a better doctor after you take a break."

Scott opened his head trauma's report and confirmed what Adam already knew—the results were normal. There was no bleeding, no swelling. All good news. They would monitor the boy's vitals and make sure he could keep food down, but that wouldn't happen in the emergency room. It was time to admit his patient and transfer the kid out of the ER.

Scott sent a message to his nurse and began the paperwork, then walked to the boy's room to give the news.

Then, under Adam's watchful eye, he walked out into the bright sunlight.

Once he was a few feet into the fresh air, his phone pinged repeatedly. That wasn't a surprise. Scott always had better reception outside the hospital. And for once, he had the energy to glance at his messages. He walked down the sidewalk and pulled his phone out of its pocket.

Scott swiped away a few emails from local businesses, and an alert that it would rain tonight.

His thumb hesitated over the single text that was left. It was from Rachel. While he hadn't texted her since the gala, Rachel had been equally silent. Scott hoped this text would bring only good news.

> Rachel
>
> Want a sandwich? My shift ends soon.
>
> I won't keep you from work. Just a quick "hi" and some food.

Scott closed his eyes, overcome with emotion. He felt touched that Rachel had thought of him. She'd forgiven him for being too busy to reach out. Hopefully, they still had a chance together.

> I'd love to see you. Food is good, too.
>
> Want to go on a boat ride Thursday? Boat leaves at 6 a.m.

Scott sighed, relieved to finally get his question out there. They'd been dancing around scheduling the boat ride for weeks. Now he just needed to wait for a response.

Scott held his breath as three little dots filled his screen. She was typing a response.

Rachel

> I'll ask my boss for Thursday off.

He grinned, standing up and stretching as he thought about Rachel's response. After texting the tour boat owner to confirm Thursday's time, he headed back inside.

"You look better," Adam noted, swinging around in Scott's desk chair. "Have a nice walk?"

"I had a great walk. Rachel texted me. We're going on that date Thursday." He scrolled through his phone, intending to add Thursday's tour to his calendar, then frowned. "I'm on call that day. Hopefully, you can handle one morning without me. I'd hate to cut my date short."

Just a few more weeks of being on call, he reminded himself. *Push through and find time with Rachel, before school starts.*

But Adam shook his head. "You're working too hard. Dr. Smith is never on call this often. You're still the only pediatric doctor here, but you don't need to carry the ER alone."

"Three more weeks…"

"No. Now. If you don't get your priorities in order, you'll miss some great things. Work shouldn't be your entire life." Adam stood up and grabbed the bag of baked goods. "I'm putting these in the break room. See you tomorrow."

Adam's words haunted him for the rest of his shift. When Rachel dropped off a sandwich, he said "goodbye" with a peck on the cheek. She'd looked happily surprised. That told Scott everything he needed to know.

At five o'clock, he headed to Human Resources for their final physician interview. It went well—if Dr. Rachel Carucci accepted their offer, she would make an excellent addition to their team.

The doctor's first name seemed like a sign.

Scott stalked down the administrative hallway, praying that William Stewart was still in the office. It was late, but not so late that all the offices were empty.

To Scott's delight, the CEO's light was on.

"Scott! How did tonight's interview go? Are we filling our last opening in the pediatric unit?" William smiled as he closed the folder in front of him, focusing his attention on Scott.

"I hope so, sir. I wasn't sure you'd still be here."

William stood up from behind his desk, then gestured toward the cushioned chairs sitting alongside the wall. "Have a seat. I took off yesterday, so I'm here late tonight. Once you're an administrator, you'll have that perk, too."

Scott nodded and sat down, then jumped up and paced the room. "I'm ready for that flexibility. That's what I'd like to talk about, actually. I came to ask a favor."

"You've earned one. What can I do?"

"I need to be pulled from Thursday's on-call schedule. And if it's possible, I'd like to transition to my new position sooner than expected." He hesitated, staring out the window of the CEO's fancy office. "I'm not quitting. But there's a special person in my life right now, and I'm going to miss a great thing if I can't spend time with her."

William raised his eyebrows, then stood and wandered back behind his desk. He picked up a photograph of his wife and turned it toward Scott. "Yesterday was my wedding anniversary. I've been in Sunset Cove for over forty years now, and she's been by my side for nearly as long. You've worked harder than I ever did. I couldn't handle being the director of a new unit *and* working full time in the emergency room." He set the picture frame back down on the desk. "We've expected too much from you. Are you ready to resign from the ER?"

"I am." Scott let out a shuttering laugh. "You warned me that tourist season was tough. You weren't kidding. I can't juggle both jobs anymore. It's time to have a life outside work."

William glanced back at the photo of his wife and smiled. "Rachel seems like a wonderful woman. You've both taken your turn at being the town hero—you deserve to be happy together. I hope things work out for you."

The two men sat down and sketched out a transition plan. By the end of the hour, it was settled. Scott would become the full-time director of pediatric medicine in two weeks. Until that time, he'd wind down his hours in the emergency room and begin distributing his old jobs to new colleagues.

Scott walked out of the hospital with a grin stretched from ear to ear. He couldn't wait to tell Rachel the news.

Chapter Thirty-One

Rachel

RACHEL LEANED BACK IN the boat seat, her dark hair whipping behind her.

"This is wonderful!" she yelled, leaning in to be closer to Scott. "I didn't think we'd go so fast."

Scott laughed and pulled her closer, wrapping an arm around Rachel. "It churns up the water and attracts more fish. That's what brings the dolphins closer," he yelled back. "They like to swim beside boats, too."

Rachel and Scott sat in silence, watching their boat cut through the water. They were headed toward the cove, a sheltered area of water that had given the town its name.

The sun had risen just a few minutes earlier. Beams of light filtered through the clouds, illuminating the sky in delicate shades of pink and orange.

Rachel snuggled closer and squealed as a wave crashed into the boat, sending a light spray of seawater their way.

"We're stopping for breakfast soon," the tour guide shouted from the helm. "Keep an eye behind the boat."

As they slowed down and entered the cove, Scott reached out and took Rachel's hand. Together they stood and walked toward the back of the boat.

"Over there!" Scott leaned closer to Rachel's ear. "Do you see them?"

Rachel gasped and pointed out to the water, still frothy from the boat's path. "There's so many dolphins! Look at them all."

She let Scott pull her closer as they watched the animals frolic in the ocean. Groups of dolphins played together, and a few babies, too. She watched with glee as their backs arched out of the water, silhouetted by a blazing sunrise.

The boat coasted to a stop less than a mile from shore. As it bobbed in the waves, the captain pulled out two boxed breakfast wraps and warm chocolate muffins from Brook's bakery. It all smelled delicious.

Scott grinned and handed Rachel her food, then helped himself to a muffin. "I have a theory," he said, chewing thoughtfully. "Brook makes her food so good that people don't want to leave. It's her secret weapon. No matter where people live, they have to return to Sunset Cove for her food."

Rachel tipped her head back and laughed. "Brook will enjoy hearing that. Did it work on you?"

"I'm staying for the food," he said, nodding and taking another bite of his muffin. Then his face broke into a smile and he nudged Rachel's shoulder. "Just joking. I've been traveling for my entire career. Always looking for a new opportunity. This seems like a good place to settle down."

Scott put down his food and reached for Rachel's hand, staring out at the sunrise.

Tears formed in Rachel's eyes as she stared out at the water, not daring to break the magic of the moment. She smiled as a pod of dolphins breached the water. Between the adults were two smaller calves. "I thought the same thing when I moved here. I didn't grow up in Sunset Cove, but it always felt I belonged here."

"Maybe we belong here together," he said, squeezing her hand and leaning down to kiss her forehead. "I'm out of the emergency room in two weeks. No more on-call hours. No more twelve-hour shifts. School starts soon, but I could work around your schedule. Lunch breaks, dinner dates. We can make this work. If that's what you want."

Rachel's heart beat faster as she considered Scott's words. After months of working together, could they finally commit to some time for themselves?

She knew they'd be good together. After all, they'd been friends for months, slowly growing closer. This could be the start of something great. "I'd like that a lot," she admitted.

Scott wrapped both arms around her in a hug, lifting her into his arms and off her feet. Rachel leaned in, soaking in the scent of salt water and the cologne she loved so much.

Then Scott put her back on her feet and grinned, shouting as a school of fish rushed underneath their boat. Their scales shimmered in the early morning sunlight. Her heart felt like it might burst from the beauty of it all—and the chance that she might finally have someone to share it with.

He leaned down to give her a kiss, lingering as if to seal their commitment to each other. Rachel hoped this kiss would be the first of many.

Then Scott pulled away, resting his forehead on hers. "I've got one more question for you."

Rachel looked up into Scott's eyes, letting herself drown in their depth. "What's that?"

He held out his arms and pulled her close, wrapping an arm around her waist and clutching her hand. "How about another dance?"

Epilogue

Scott smiled as he looked around his new office. The first stage of the children's wing would open in a few days. They were right on schedule.

It had taken the work of the entire community—and one determined music teacher—to bring them to this point. Scott had much to be grateful for. Every night, he gave thanks for having Rachel in his life. She'd helped him build a hospital and a new life.

He grinned as Rachel knocked on his office door and stuck in her head. "Can I come in? I brought lunch."

"You're always welcome here." Scott stood up from his desk and wrapped his arms around Rachel, wondering again how he'd gotten so lucky. They had dated for almost two months now, and knew they were perfect for each other—crazy work schedules and all. They'd finally found balance when they found each other.

Rachel hefted a paper bag onto the desk and unpacked her food. Sandwiches, cupcakes, brownies, and little bags of chips soon sat in a line, waiting to be chosen.

Scott stared at the feast in front of them. "Were you hungry today?"

She tipped her head back and laughed. "Brook baked too much. We're sharing the leftovers with the construction crew upstairs. She wanted to sneak food to her fiance."

Rachel's heart warmed as she thought about Brook and Brad's wedding this spring. She was glad her friends had picked a date.

Rachel was also thrilled to have a plus-one for the wedding. Life was more fun when you had someone to share it with.

She folded the bakery's paper bag, then realized that Scott was still watching her. "Is this okay? I'll pack up the leftovers when we're done. And I won't stay too long. You're busy getting ready for the opening."

But Scott just continued to watch her, a smile slowly growing on his face. "You're always welcome here. It's nice to share a break with someone. Besides, the other doctors and nurses bring their wives and kids to work."

"I'm not your wife," she pointed out. "There's a difference between a wife and girlfriend. I don't want you to get in trouble."

Scott reached for her hand and pulled her toward the couch. "You've never caused me trouble."

"Even with a broken arm?" she laughed. "I caused lots of trouble with my broken arm."

He gave her a teasing grin. "Between the two of us and three good arms, we got things done. But back to being my girlfriend..." Scott leaned in for a long kiss, then moved away.

"I wasn't done kissing," she protested. "But we should eat. We both need to get back to work."

"Work can wait, and I think you'll enjoy this more," he said, sinking down to one knee.

Rachel's heart thudded painfully as Scott reached into his pocket and pulled out a small velvet box.

He clasped Rachel's hands and looked her in the eyes, a grin stretching across his face. "Rachel Marie Lancaster, I love you and can't wait to spend the rest of my life with you. Will you marry me?"

Rachel gasped as he revealed a princess-cut diamond surrounded by purple gems. He'd remembered her favorite color—and picked out a ring as beautiful and unique as their relationship. She fought back tears as she nodded and tried to smile. "Yes. Yes. A hundred times, yes! I'd love to marry you."

The couple snuggled together on the couch, the food all but forgotten. "I hope you like the ring," he murmured. "You don't seem like a diamond band type of girl. I wanted something fun, and beautiful, and magical, just like you."

She held out her hand, twisting it left and right to catch the light. "It's all that and more. But I don't care about the ring. I care about you. I can't wait to start our life together."

Scott leaned in for a quick kiss and nodded. "I thought I was too busy to fall in love, but you proved me wrong. You're the best thing that's ever happened to me."

Rachel snuggled closer, content to sit in Scott's arms as long as possible. Work could wait for at least a few more minutes.

Unfortunately, it couldn't wait forever. She was about to stand up and grab some food when there was a knock.

"Come in," Scott called, untangling his arms from Rachel's. "The door's open."

William Steward walked through the door with a grin. "How's our new director of pediatric medicine? Settling in to your office?" He glanced around the room and gave Rachel a warm smile. "I see you've got lunch covered, both the food and the company."

Scott stood to shake his CEO's hand. "I'm nearly unpacked. Rachel brought enough food for us and half the construction crew. You're welcome to join us if you're hungry."

Rachel nodded in agreement, pleased that William was happy to see her. Scott had some wonderful co-workers. They'd welcomed her with open arms at the company picnic. She could understand why Scott was ready to settle down and commit to Sunset Cove's hospital—and grateful to the people who had helped him make that decision. "Yes, please stay! We've got enough food for twenty people here."

William shook his head, but walked over to the desk and picked up a brownie. He carefully wrapped it in a napkin. "I can't stay long. I'm just here to talk about Christmas."

Scott's brow furrowed. "It's early October."

"That's right. There's not much time to plan!" William nodded toward the calendar on Scott's desk. "This will be our first Christmas with a children's ward. We should celebrate."

To Rachel's surprise, Scott shook his head and held up his hands. "Oh, no. It's Adam's turn to take charge," he announced. "I'll help him sketch out ideas, but I've got a wedding to plan."

William's eyes lit up with delight as Rachel held out her hand. "That's wonderful! I'll let Adam know. He can dress up as Santa Claus and hand out gifts for the children. I'm sure he'll be in touch."

Scott chuckled as his boss walk out of the office. He grabbed a plate and filled it with two sandwiches and a pile of cookies, then sat on the couch with Rachel and balanced the plate between them. "Adam will make a great Santa, and I know exactly who he'll ask for help. But let's talk about us for a few more minutes. Did you have a wedding date in mind?"

Rachel smiled as she broke off a piece of cookie. "We'll have to plan around the school schedule, but summer break is over. I don't want to wait an entire year."

"Neither do I." Scott reached out to squeeze her hand. "How long is your Christmas break?"

"I'll have two weeks off." She set her food down and grinned at Scott, an idea forming in her head. "Would that work? If we keep things simple, we could get married over Christmas break."

"I like the way you think." Scott leaned in for another kiss. "I know someone with a house in Paris. We can celebrate the New Year in France."

Rachel laughed, shaking her head at how quickly things were falling into place. "As long as you're there, France sounds like a wonderful place to be."

Spend more time in Sunset Cove!

Adam Locke and Emma Miller are in charge of the hospital's Christmas toy drive, and Adam is determined to win Emma's heart before they ring in the new year.

Who needs luck when you've got mistletoe?

Immerse yourself in the holiday spirit by reading Christmas in Sunset Cove!

About the Author

Tori Mitchell writes sweet, small-town romance with a guaranteed Happily Ever After.

She found her own small-town happy ending in the Pocono Mountains of Pennsylvania, where she lives with her husband and two children. When she's not reading, writing or daydreaming about the beach, you'll find Tori growing an absurd amount of tomatoes and rhubarb in her garden.

Get the latest news on sales, new books, and more with Tori's newsletter at subscribepage.io/ToriMitchellnewsletter.

Join the Kindness Committee!

THANK YOU FOR READING *Hometown Hero in Sunset Cove.* If you enjoyed Rachel and Scott's story, please consider leaving a review on Amazon or Goodreads. Even a short review can help us reach new readers and spread more kindness.

How does a story spread kindness? **If you purchased this book, you've officially joined the Sunset Cove Kindness Committee!** Ten percent of profits from the Sunset Cove series are donated to non-profit organizations like the Child Life program at Children's Hospital of Philadelphia, which helps children facing a serious illness or hospitalization.

Printed in Great Britain
by Amazon

60951808R00119